To Marit and Mona

TO SIBERIA

Per Petterson

TO SIBERIA

Translated from the Norwegian
by Anne Born

THE HARVILL PRESS
LONDON

First published in Norway with the title *Til Sibir*
by Oktober Forlag, Oslo, in 1996

First published in Great Britain in 1998 by
The Harvill Press
2 Aztec Row, Berners Road
London N1 0PW

www.harvill-press.com

3 5 7 9 8 6 4 2

A CIP catalogue record for this book
is available from the British Library

This translation has been published
with the financial support of NORLA

ISBN 1 86046 460 2

Designed and typeset in StonePrint at
Libanus Press, Marlborough, Wiltshire

Printed and bound in Germany by Ebner Ulm GmbH

TO SIBERIA

I

When I was a little girl of six or seven I was always scared when we passed the lions on our way out of town. I was sure Lucifer felt as I did, for he always put on speed at that very place. I did not realise until much later it was because my grandfather whipped him up sharply on the way down the gentle slope past the gateway where the lions were, and *that* was because Grandfather was an impatient man. It was a well known fact.

The lions were yellow and I sat at the rear of the trap dangling my legs, alone or with my brother Jesper, with my back towards Grandfather, watching the lions diminishing up there. They turned their heads and stared at me with yellow eyes. They were made of stone, as were the plinths they lay on, but all the same their staring made my chest burn and gave me a hollow feeling inside. I could not take my eyes off them. Each time I tried to look down at the gravelled road instead, I turned dizzy and felt I was falling.

"They're coming! They're coming!" shouted my brother, who knew all about those lions, and I looked up again and saw them coming. They tore themselves free of the stone blocks and grew larger, and I jumped off the trap heedless of the speed, grazed my knees on the gravel and ran out into the nearest field. There were roedeer and stags in the forest beyond the field, and I thought about that as I ran.

"Can't you leave the lass alone!" bellowed my grandfather. I stopped running, there was dew on the grass and my ankles were wet, I felt stubble and stalks and rough ground under my bare feet. Grandfather pulled in the reins and shouted at the horse and the trap came to a halt; he turned round and out of his beard a stream of oaths as foul as the devil himself could utter poured over Jesper's head. My grandfather was a man full of wrath and in the end I always had to stand up for my brother, for there was no way I could live without him.

I walked across the grass to the road again, climbed on to the trap and smiled at Jesper. Grandfather cracked the whip and Lucifer moved off and Jesper smiled back.

I walk the same road with my father. It is Christmas time. I am nine years old. It is unusually cold today, hoar frost and leafless poplars line the fields beside the road. Something grey moves at the grey edge of the forest, the thin legs of deer step stiffly and frosty mist comes in puffs from their soft muzzles, I can see it though I'm a long way away. You could touch the air, like glass, and everything seems very close. I am wearing my cap and scarf, my hands are thrust deep into my coat pockets. There is a hole in one, I can feel the lining on the inside. Now and then I look up at him. There's a bulge at the top of his back, almost like a hump. He got that out in the fields and he is never going back there, he says. My father is a carpenter in town,

Grandfather gave him a workshop when he left the farm.

He grits his teeth. He is bare-headed and he looks straight in front of him with red-rimmed eyes, his ears are white with frost and I can't stop looking at them. They are like porcelain. His arm rises and stops before it gets right up, and he almost forces it down again. When we are halfway I take my hand out of my pocket to hold his, and he takes it without looking down and squeezes it lightly, but I am doing it because *he* is the one who is cold.

When we pass the lions we don't turn to look at them, he because he is just looking straight ahead anyway and I because I do not want to. We are going out to the farm. My mother is there already, and my uncles and Jesper are there, and my father walks stiffly and does not hurry. We have come three kilometres from town, it is the 24th December and then I turn round after all. The lions lie on their plinths covered with greyish white shining ice. Yesterday it rained and then came the frost, and now they are caged and look like my father's ears, two porcelain lions on guard before the avenue leading to Bangsbo Manor where Hans Christian Andersen stayed when he came as far north as this, the tall hat in the low rooms, a black streak of a man who always had to bend his head, on his way in, on his way out.

I try to walk faster, I am worried about his ears, I have heard they can fall off, but he keeps on at the same speed. I pull him by the arm and then he gets cross.

"Stop that, can't you!" he snaps and pulls me back in place roughly and this is the first thing he has said since we stepped out of the door in Asylgade. My father is fond of Jesper. I am fond of my father. Jesper is fond of me, but he likes to tease me, frighten me in the dark with death's heads, pull me under water in the summer. I can stand it, it makes me feel like him. I am walking alone with my father, it is Christmas and his ears are made of porcelain. I'm afraid they will fall off and he does not touch them the whole five kilometres to the farm.

There are four farms in Vrangbæk and they are all called Vrangbæk, it is quite a small village. There are some children there, they go to Vangen School in Understed. I might have been one of them, but I'm not, and "You should be glad about that," Jesper always tells me. We turn down left at the crossroads where the road straight ahead winds across the fields to Gærum and the one to the right goes up to North Vrangbæk. We pass the first barn of stone and brick, my father walks if anything still slower and more stiffly and keeps a firm hold on my hand. The road takes a sharp bend with a steep slope on one side paved with round stones at the lowest point, it looks like a stone wall but is there to stop the earth sliding on to the road after rain and barring the way. We are going to the last farm, they are close together and near the road, so you can just walk straight into the big cobbled yard with the dung heap in the middle. Everything is glazed with a layer of shining ice. The cobblestones leading to the door are slippery.

The first person I catch sight of is Jesper, he has seen us from the window. He stands waiting at the living-room door. Behind him I see the Christmas tree and the window on the opposite side with frost flowers halfway up the panes. It looks pretty. I hear my mother's voice. She is a Christian, her voice is Christian. She has one foot on earth and one in heaven. Jesper smiles as if we share a secret. Maybe we do, I do not remember. My father goes straight over to the big tiled stove. It is rumbling, I can see it is hot because the air around it quivers and I feel it on my face and he goes so close I'm afraid he is going to press his forehead to the tiles. I take off my coat and he lifts his arms like a puppet on a string and presses his hands to his ears. In the living room my mother sings "Chime ye bells", and Jesper gazes at me and over at the man standing in front of the stove. I hold my coat in my arms and see his crooked back and jutting jawbones and the white frosty vapour running out between his fingers.

The attic at the farm was icy cold and usually in half darkness with only one paraffin lamp I had to turn off as soon as I had gone up the stairs. There was a small window on the east side and the bed was under the window and kneeling on it I could talk to Jesper in the evenings when it was summer time and look out at the stars in winter and a spruce hedge and a Chinese garden from another world and then just rolling fields right out to the sea. Sometimes in the night I would wake up under the coarse heavy duvet thinking I had heard the sea filling the room, and I opened my eyes and it was just as dark as when I shut them again. The darkness lay close to my face and I thought, it doesn't make any difference whether I can see or not. But there *was* a difference, and I would be frightened, for the darkness was big and heavy and full of sounds and I knew if I did not shut my eyes quickly I would be smothered. But when I wasn't frightened it was like being lifted up to float in space with a wind through my heart.

I lie in bed looking into the dark and everything is black and then it turns grey, for the moon has come out. I can't hear the sea. It is frozen like everything else, frozen and quiet. I do not think I am dreaming any more.

Someone is knocking. That is why I woke up, I remember now. I wait and the knocking comes again and I get up from under the duvet which has warmed through at last and walk across the cold floor in my nightdress to where I know the door is. More knocking. It is not the door, it's the window. I turn round and see a shadow moving against the moonlight in front of the window. It is Jesper. I know it's Jesper.

"Let me in," he whispers loudly, breathing warmth on the glass. I run over to the bed and jump up on to it knees first and open the window. A cold gust rushes in, it chills my chest and stomach and my thoughts turn sharp at the edges. I remember everything, the porcelain lions and porcelain ears and Grandmother's straight neck and Grandfather and my mother's frail voice fluttering in the room like a thin veil we all tend to ignore. Jesper hangs on to the eaves with one hand and has one foot on the window sill. He has my boots around his neck with the laces knotted behind his head.

"Get dressed and come with me," he says.

"All right," I say.

I have a will of my own, I do not do everything I'm told, but I *want* to be with Jesper. He does things that are original, I like that and I am wide awake now. He swings himself in and sits on the bed waiting and he smiles the whole time. I hurry to put my clothes on. They are lying on a chair and they're very cold. The moon shines in through the open window and makes silver circles on the bedposts, on a pitcher, on an alarm clock whose hands have always stood still.

"What's the time?" I ask.

"Haven't a clue." He smiles so his teeth shine in the semi-darkness. I start laughing, but then he puts his finger to his lips. I nod and do the same and then I find my woollen underwear and pull it on and the heavy skirt and a sweater. I have brought my coat up to my room with me, it hangs over the chair back. Jesper hands me my boots, and when I am ready we climb out.

"Don't be scared, just do what I do," he says.

I'm not scared, and I just do what he does, it is not difficult when we do it in time with each other, he goes first and I follow, it is like a dance only the two of us know and we dance along the roof until we come to the end where a birch reaches up with strong branches and there we climb down. Jesper goes first, and I follow him.

We keep away from the road and the wing where the grown-ups' bedrooms are and go through the Chinese garden in the moonlight to get out into the fields. There are narrow paths and frozen shrubs and dead flowers in the garden and a winding artificial stream with frozen water, and there are several little wooden bridges across the stream. Carp swim in the stream in summer and maybe they are still there, underneath the ice. As we cross the bridges the woodwork creaks so loudly I am afraid it will wake the people in the house. When the moon goes behind a cloud I stop and wait.

"Jesper, wait," I call softly, but he does not wait before he is through the garden and into the first field. Then he turns round and there is moonlight again and I catch up with him.

We walk across the fields, at first we wind upwards and then down on the other side till we can see the sea and we throw shadows as we walk. I have never been outside like this, never had a shadow at night. My coat is lit up in front by the moon and Jesper's back is completely dark. When we stop and look out over the ice it is white at first and then shining and then just the open sea.

Jesper takes something from his pocket and puts it in his mouth and lights a match. And then he blows out. There is a scent of cigar. He says:

"It won't be long before I'm going to do what Ernst Bremer did. Get hold of a fast boat and go to Sweden and come back with enough booze for everyone who wants to to get really drunk. I shall make money and smoke cigars. But *I* shall only drink on Saturdays. And then only two glasses."

Jesper is twelve. Ernst Bremer is a smuggler. He is the greatest of them all and everyone knows who he is. A short man from Gothenburg who has a house in the street beyond ours where he stays when no one is after him. I have seen him walk past in a grey coat, with his dark hair parted in the middle and sometimes wearing a beret. He has been in the papers lots of times, once with a drawing by Storm Petersen showing him cocking a snook at the customs officers, and when the boys are out in the evening they do not play cops and robbers, but Ernst Bremer and customs men. He is better than Robin Hood. My father bought a bottle off him one summer, but when my mother realised where it came from she made him pour it out on to the flower bed. None of the flowers died, although she said it was poison.

Jesper blows grey smoke at the sea, and then he coughs and spits.

"Phoo!" he says, "but I'll need some practice first."

My mother is velvet, my mother is iron. My father often stays silent and sometimes over dinner he picks up the burning hot pan by its iron handle and holds it until I have filled my plate, and when he puts it back I can see the red marks on his hand.

"Hans Christian Andersen stayed at Bangsbo," I say although I know Jesper knows this and he says:

"I know," and we walk beside the water for a while and up a steep dune and back again across the fields. We have the moon on our backs and the shadow is in front and that is worse straight away. I don't like it even though I see the house clearly when we get to the top. It is dark down the slope. The wind is getting up, I keep my hand on one cheek, for it is freezing, then some clouds start to gather and I can barely see. We go round the garden instead of through it and come up to the house where the barn stands at an angle, and Jesper goes right across to the barn alongside the spruce hedge and puts his face to the nearest window. The whitewashed walls are as murky as fog, and he shades his eyes with one hand as if there were reflections and sunlight outside, but it is dark and I can't see what he is looking at and he says:

"Jesus Christ, Grandfather has hanged himself in the cowshed."

"No!" I cry and cannot think why he chose to say just that, but I have often thought about it since, in all the years that have passed until now.

"Yes," he says, "come over and see." I don't want to see, I feel sick even though I know it is not true, but still I run over and put my face beside his. It's completely dark, I can't see anything.

"I can't see anything. You haven't seen anything, it's all dark." I press my face to the pane, there is a smell of cowshed in there, there is a smell of cold and Jesper starts to chuckle. Suddenly I feel how cold it is.

"I'm freezing."

"We'll go in then," he says, and stops laughing.

"I don't want to go in yet. It's colder inside. I won't be able to sleep either."

"I mean into the cowshed. It's warm there."

We go round the barn over the cobbles as far as the cowshed door. It creaks when we open it and I wonder if Grandfather is hanging there, perhaps I shall walk straight into his legs, perhaps they'll swing to and fro. But he is not hanging there and it's suddenly warmer,

14

the smell is a smell I know. Jesper goes in among the stalls. There are a lot of them, there are twenty-five cows, it is not a small farm, they have labourers. Grandmother had worked in the kitchen before she was married to Grandfather. She wore a white apron then but she has never done so since. She is mother to my father, not to his brothers, and no time was wasted before that wedding once Hedvig was in her grave, so my mother told us. Grandmother and Grandfather are hardly ever in the same room together, and when they are Grand-mother holds her head high and her neck stiff. Everyone can see it.

I stand there getting used to the heavy darkness. I hear Jesper's steps inside and the cows shifting about in the stalls, and I know without seeing them that most of them are lying down, they're sleeping, they're chewing, they bump their horns against the low dividing walls and fill the darkness with deep sounds.

"Come on then," says Jesper, and now I can see him right at the end, and I walk softly down the middle past the stalls, careful not to tread in the muck along the sides of the walkway. Jesper laughs quietly and starts to sing about those who walk the narrow path and not the broad road towards the pearly gates in the blue, and he mimics my mother's voice and he does it so well I would have burst out laughing, but dared not in the presence of all these animals.

"Come on now, Sistermine," says Jesper, and then I step all the way up to where he is and he takes hold of my coat. "Are you still cold?"

"A bit."

"Then you must do this," he says, enters one of the stalls and pushes his way in between the wall and the cow lying there. He squats down and strokes her back and talks in a low voice I do not often hear him use, and she turns her head and edges nervously towards the far wall, but then she quietens down. He strokes her harder and harder and then cautiously lies down on her back, quite stiff at first and when he feels it is safe he goes limp and just lies there like a big dark patch on the patched cow. "Big animals have a lot of heat," he says, "like a stove, you try it." His voice is sleepy, and I do not know if I can manage, but now I'm sleepy too, so sleepy that if I don't lie down soon I shall fall over.

"Try the next stall," says Jesper, "that's Dorit, she's friendly."

I stand in the walkway and hear Jesper breathing calmly and look in at Dorit in her stall until her broad back stands out clearly and then I take a big step over the gutter but not quite big enough, but now I don't care, I'm too sleepy. I bend down and stroke Dorit's back.

"You have to say something, you must talk to her," says Jesper from behind the wall, but I do not know what to say, all the ideas I think of are things I cannot say aloud. It is cramped in the stall, if Dorit turns round I shall be squeezed against the wall. I stroke her neck and lean forward more and start to tell the story of the steadfast tin soldier into her ear, and she listens and I know Jesper is listening behind the wall. When I reach the end where the tin soldier bursts into flames and is melting, I lie

16

down on her and put my arms around her neck and tell her how the puff of wind comes in at the window and lifts up the ballerina and carries her through the room into the fire where she flares up like a shooting star and dies out, and when I have finished I dare not breathe. But Dorit is amiable, she hardly moves, just chews and the warmth of her body spreads through my coat, I feel it on my stomach and slowly I start to breathe again. It is Christmas Eve 1934 and Jesper and I lie there each in our stall each on our own cow in a cowshed where all things breathe and perhaps we fall asleep, for I do not remember anything very clearly after that.

2

The town we lived in was a provincial one at that time, in the far north of the country, almost as far as it was possible to travel from Copenhagen and still have streets to walk along. But we had earthworks going back two hundred years, and a shipyard with more than a hundred workers and a lunch-break siren that could be heard all over the town at noon. We had a harbour for fishing boats where the throbbing of the trawlers' motors never stopped, and boats came in from the capital, from Sweden and from Norway. If you took the swaying wooden staircase to Pikkerbakken up from Møllehuset and stood by the viewpoint at the top, you could see the sea like an enormous painting when the big boats turned in towards the two lighthouses on the breakwater. From the height of Pikkerbakken the sea looked as if it *hung* rather than lay.

I remember how we stood on the quay watching the swells go down the gangway from the Copenhagen boat. They had travelled first class and now they were going to Frydenstrand health resort for the bathing or further on to Skagen by train to rent holiday houses or stay at hotels for the summer weeks. The men wore straw boaters and the ladies' dresses were bright in the sunshine. The upper-class people of Copenhagen had just discovered

Skagen and a special railway line ran from the harbour to take them to the station although it was only a few blocks away. I watched porters in uniform carrying their suitcases over to the train, and I thought it might be an aim in life, to have someone to carry your suitcases for you.

When the boats came in we could hear them hooting from a long way away, and then my father would take off his carpenter's apron and hang it on a nail behind the workshop door and walk through the streets to the harbour to see them arrive. He always walked at the same pace and never hurried, he knew exactly how long it took. He would stop a few metres from the edge of the quay, and there he stayed in the long coat he always wore when it was windy, with his hands clasped behind his back and his brown beret on his head, but it was not possible to see what he was thinking, for his face was so calm and he only went there when the boats came in and never when they left, unless there was someone on board he knew, and that was seldom the case.

When I was not at school we both stood there. I too had my hands behind my back and the wind pulled at his coat and the wind pulled at my hair and whirled it around so it whipped both him and me. It was a mass of brown hair with ringlets that bounced against my back when I ran. Many people in town said it looked nice, even dashing, but I felt it just got in the way, and when I suggested cutting it short my mother said "No, for it's your best feature and without it you'd look like an Eskimo because of your round face." According to her the Eskimos were a race who lived at the North Pole and worshipped gods of blubber and bone and unfortunately Denmark ruled over them. But everyone has their cross to bear, and I had not the strength in those days to defy her, so I used to pull my hair back tightly with a rubber band at the neck so I could take part in all Jesper's projects. The latest one was Great Discoveries. He would get together with some friends and they would roam the roads and the forests of the neighbourhood and in the evenings they would meet in a cellar on the other side of the Plantation where one of them lived and make plans for The Great Journey. I was the only girl allowed to be with them now and then.

But I enjoyed the feeling of the wind in my hair, and I knew my father liked to see it blow straight out when we stood on the quay and watched the boats come in. And after all it was my only pride.

The train waited behind us, puffing and hissing through its valves, and even though it was only an hour's journey to Skagen, I had never been there.

"Can't we go to Skagen one day?" I asked. Being with Jesper and his friends had made me realise the world was far bigger than the town I lived in and the fields around it, and I wanted to go travelling and see it.

"There's nothing but sand at Skagen," my father said, "you don't want to go there, my lass." And because it was Sunday and he seldom said *my lass*, he took a cigar from his waistcoat pocket with a pleased expression, lit it and blew out smoke into the wind. The smoke flew back in our faces and scorched them, but I pretended not to notice and so did he. With smarting eyes we watched the passenger boat *Melchior* approach the opening in the breakwater full steam ahead, tears streamed and I squeezed my eyelids into narrow cracks. All along one side of the deck the passengers hung over the rail waving their handkerchiefs, the *Melchior* swung round and slackened speed, and there came the tugboat, fixed the hawser on board and moved off with engines roaring and the hawser snapped out of the water so the spray leapt up and the drops sparkled in the sun. The big boat turned gently in towards the quay where people stood waiting in groups, and someone on land called:

"Have you been seasick?"

"YEEES!" yelled the whole row in chorus.

When all the passengers had landed and the ones who were going by train were settled and the train had left, we turned away from the wind, dried our eyes and went back into town. Then we crossed the street leading from the cobbled jetty towards the Cimbria Hotel and round the hotel to Lodsgade with Consul Broch's house on the right and Færgekroen, the Ferry Inn, on the left and right along Danmarksgade to the corner where our street, Asylgade, joined it. We stopped there, and he said:

"That's all for the two of us today. Go home to your mother now." He was strict about not having me along too much although he knew I would rather be with him. But I had to go home and soon I would hear all about the priest's sermon that day and about the whole service, while my father went on to Aftenstjernen, the Evening Star, to play billiards with his friends as it was Sunday.

The first time I do remember us going to Skagen was in autumn. Grandfather at Vrangbæk had just turned sixty-five, and everyone had been out to the farm, the whole family with uncles and aunts and people from the neighbouring farms. The sun came in through the windows, the rooms were full of people, and some were out in the farmyard and among the shrubs in the Chinese garden, yet all the same the day was filled with clinking silence and stiff necks. Grandmother walked about in her white apron for the first time in forty years, she served drinks from a tray and smiled in a way that made Grandfather sit in his chair as if paralysed and my father stand up all day long, and not once did their eyes meet. My mother's voice was more fluting than usual and even though there were many guests, hers was the one I kept hearing.

But at Skagen we found the tourists had gone back to Copenhagen for the winter. Not a fine dress to be seen in the main street, not a straw hat or parasol, and even though I knew we were making this trip for my sake, I was disappointed. My father was right, there was not much there except sand. The wild wind swept right down among the low yellow houses whose owners stayed inside behind closed doors, my mother held on to her hat and Jesper walked sideways with his back to the wind, and it was blowing so hard out at Grenen, where the two seas meet at the tip of the sand spit, that we could not go out there with horses as we had planned, and sand and salt stuck in my hair, my clothes, my mouth when I wanted to speak and it was difficult to walk without feeling it smarting between the thighs.

What I liked was the train ride. It took an hour and that was enough for me to be able to lean backwards against the seat with closed eyes, feel the joints in the rails come up and thump through my body and sometimes peer out of the windows and see windswept heathland and imagine I was on the Trans-Siberian Railway. I had read about it, seen pictures in a book and decided that no matter when and how life would turn out, one day I would travel from Moscow to Vladivostok on that train, and I practised saying the names: Omsk, Tomsk, Novosibirsk, Irkutsk, they were difficult to pronounce with all their hard consonants, but ever since the trip to Skagen, every journey I made by train was a potential departure on my own great journey.

Jesper was heading for Morocco. That would be too hot for me. I wanted open skies that were cold and clear, where it was easy to breathe and easy to see for long distances, but his pictures were mysterious and alluring in black and white with barren mountains in the far distance and sun-scorched faces and sun-scorched towns behind battlemented walls and fluttering tunics and palm trees that suddenly rose out of no-man's-land.

"I'll get there if I want to," said Jesper. "And I do want to." He looked at the pictures and maps in his book and read aloud:

"Marrakech, Fez, Meknès, Kasba." He shaped his mouth to the vowels and held on to them and in his voice they turned into magic spells and we promised each other that this was something we would achieve. He fetched a knife and we made cuts in our hands and mixed the blood that had been mixed before, but now it would be like a circle, said Jesper.

We stood in the shed behind the house holding each other's hands, it was almost too solemn, Jesper did not laugh as usual, my palm hurt, and I could hear the rain on the corrugated iron roof and in the trees outside and beyond the rain was a silence so huge it filled the whole of Denmark.

But at Skagen the wind was deafening and it thumped at everything out on the road where we walked huddled together like a family in a newspaper pictured fleeing from cannons. We had tried everywhere but there was nowhere to take shelter. The kiosks were closed because of bad weather, the cafés were never open on Sunday and in the harbour the waves were breaking on shore. And *then* it began to rain. It came from all directions at full speed and not *on* us, but *against* us with the wind right in our faces; we tried to turn away, walk sideways so as not to drown and Jesper gave up and ran out into the middle of the road and began to dance with his arms in the air.

"Come and see! Come and see! The people from heaven have come to conquer the new world. Come and see! Come and see!" he shouted, laughing for joy. The rain streamed from his hair and in several windows the curtains were drawn aside and there stood the occupants gaping out while they moved their lips at someone beyond them in the shadows and shook their heads.

"Come and see your superiors!" shouted Jesper. "We

have pearls of glass and swords of steel!"

"Keep your mouth shut, boy!" roared my father, "get back to your place!" He had water in his eyes and water in his voice, and Jesper replied:

"Woof, woof," and panted like a dog and joined the flock again, and we went on down the road to the railway station. We tottered into the station building where the man in the ticket office told us that our train would not leave for about three hours. He looked at us sideways under his cap, he was used to finer folk. The whole trip collapsed like a house of cards. We huddled together under the the platform roof, my father bit the inside of his cheeks until they bulged and gazed into the air and had nothing to say. He had planned it all and it had not turned out as he had intended and now we were trapped here. My mother pulled her shawl more tightly around her shoulders and I thought it did not matter that I was disappointed. After all, the only thing wrong with this journey was that it was too short.

When we walk down Asylgade on our way from the station Lucifer is standing in front of the house. I can still feel the train in my body, and the wind and the yellow houses, my long hair is done up in a plait my mother made and it feels sticky, full of sand and salt rain and stiff as a rope. I fiddle with it and try to loosen it, but it's impossible without help. Lucifer is not tied up, he walks across the road and nibbles the grass at the edge of the gravel of a house on the other side, with the trap in tow. No one but Grandfather drives Lucifer, but Uncle Nils is sitting on the steps with his head in his hands, he is wearing his black Sunday jacket and working trousers covered with big stains and clogs on his feet. We are all cold and walking quicker than usual, and when Uncle Nils catches sight of us he gets up with his arms straight down by his sides and his fists clenched. He opens them and clenches them again. I see my father looking at his hands and he looks at the horse.

"Something's happened," says Jesper.

"Shut up, boy," says my father.

My mother turns. "But Magnus!"

"Shut up, I say."

I take his hand, but he doesn't notice and does not hold mine. Uncle Nils is white in the face even though he works out in the fields south of Vrangbæk most of the year. "Grandfather is dead," he tells us. "He has hanged himself in the cowshed." We stand quite still. We should not be hearing this, Jesper and I, and I do not look at him, I see the cowshed with the stalls in a row in the half darkness and all the beams in there and Dorit lying in her stall chewing with her big warm body against my coat, and I get warm thinking of it even though the wind cuts icily down Asylgate and I am so freezing my teeth chatter, but all the same I don't feel cold.

"Come on," says Jesper, "we'll go in." He pulls me by the arm towards the door where my mother is already on her way inside. She sings a song quietly to herself and goes into the kitchen, lowers the blanket of hymn between herself and us, and Jesper and I go into the living room and stand at the window looking out on to the road. Uncle Nils holds my father by his coat, looking down at the ground as he talks fast, we can hear his voice but not what he says. My father knocks his hand away and crosses the road to Lucifer and gets hold of his bridle. Lucifer pulls back and rears on his hind legs, my father holds on and is pulled upwards so he has to stand on tiptoe on only one foot and Uncle Nils goes running up to them on clattering clogs. Together they calm the horse down enough for them to climb into the trap, and my father takes the reins. Lucifer rears again and my father yells so his voice slams hard and cold against the house walls and Lucifer sets off at a trot down the road. The last thing we see is my father's brown beret before they vanish round the corner and off down Danmarksgade on their way out of town towards Vrangbæk.

"How could I have known that?" says Jesper. "I couldn't know it."

"Of course you couldn't."

"Maybe I've got dark powers. Maybe I can look into the future and see disasters to come, like Sara in the forest."

But Sara in the forest is an old lady who lives in an old house at the edge of the woods beside the road to Vrangbæk, and Jesper is not like her at all. She can read coffee grounds and read your palm, she knows the names of all the stars and plants and what they can be used for, and some say she killed her own child because it didn't have a father. She had never been with a man so what she gave birth to was no human child.

She is Jesper's favourite spook and he always shouts "She's coming! She's coming!" and I step on my pedals as hard as I can when we cycle past there in the evening. She can see through the dark, Jesper thinks.

"I don't think anyone can do that. You're always imagining things. Everyone knows that."

3

But that was not all. When they cut Grandfather down they found a scrap of paper in his jacket pocket. He was wearing a white shirt and his best suit with watch chain and waistcoat, his thick hair was brushed back like shining fur, and there was no grey in it, because he had eaten bones and gristle all his life. His beard was gone, and the men who found him said he looked naked and ten years younger, and I have wondered whether they really saw him straight away in there. For it was dark and early morning and they might have brushed against his legs so he swung to and fro with a creaking sound from the beam in the quiet byre with the row of cow's rumps. And was Dorit standing up in her stall, or lying in the straw chewing the cud, and did she know the man who owned her was hanging there on a rope from the ceiling with a scrap of paper in his pocket?

The paper was folded twice without a speck on it and bore a note in his handwriting: *I cannot go on any longer.* I was sure that was something we understood, both Jesper and I, that he could not go on any longer, but what it was he could not go on with we had no idea, because he was as strong as an ox and could work harder and longer than anyone else I have ever known.

**

Once a month he harnessed Lucifer to the trap and set off at a trot into town, and then no one else was allowed to go with him. It was always on the same day, he had done it for years, and the route he took never varied either. He was known to many people in the town and they saluted him with their hands to their caps as if he was a general and some sneered openly after he had gone by. But Lucifer trotted up the hill past Bangsbo with the lions at the gates, past Møllehuset Allé, gravel spurted from under the wheels all the way along Søndergade where the fishermen's houses lay close together down to the shore, and all the lights were on in the Mission House. And perhaps someone in the doorway stood there staring and thought, Dear God, preserve us from the deluge when that comes, but it was Grandfather coming and he did not greet anyone. Lucifer just kept on trotting through the town along Danmarksgade, across the church square, past the Løveapotek and past our road where I stood on the corner in my coat, waiting and stamping my feet to keep warm. I had been waiting a good while and finally he came, sitting big and stiff in the trap behind the horse on his way to the Aftenstjernen to get drunk. That was the first place he stopped at, with a thick rubber band round his wallet. I had seen that wallet. The rubber band was red, and when he had taken some money out and was folding the wallet up again, he held the rubber band between thumb and fingers and slapped it back with a snap that was *meant* to be heard.

Lucifer's hooves clattered on the cobblestones, but there was no need to hide, Grandfather never looked to the side, and I was freezing and pushed my hands up the sleeves of my coat like a muff, and if he had seen me he would not have recognised me, because he didn't really *see* anything.

I gazed after the trap after it had gone behind the houses on Nytorv, and as I turned to go home Jesper was standing right behind me in the shadows, grey jacket, grey trousers, only his eyes were shining. He looked up the road where Grandfather had disappeared and said:

"That's a hundred kroner gone for sure."

"Have you been here long?"

"As long as you have. You're not the only one who knows what day it is."

I pulled the collar of my coat round my ears and turned to look up the road again.

"He's going to the Aftenstjernen," I said.

"Mm. And then he'll go on to the Færgekroen and the Vinkælderen and Tordenskjold's Kro."

"And to end with he'll go to the bar at the Cimbria Hotel," I said.

"And there he'll be chucked out because he can't stand on his feet, and then he'll stumble out to the trap and slump on the seat and fall asleep while Lucifer trots all the way to Vrangbæk, and if he doesn't fall out he'll get home instead of freezing to death."

"He did fall out once."

"But that was in summer and the whole town saw him lying in the ditch snoring with his face in his own vomit. Ugh. And tomorrow he won't speak to Grandmother."

"He never does that anyway."

"Shall we go after him and watch?"

"We've done that before. It's no fun, it's horrible, and I'm freezing."

"You always are. But I've brought your gloves, and cap and scarf," said Jesper. And so he had, hidden behind his back in a bundle. He held it out saying:

"You must plan things, Sistermine, you must think it out beforehand," but I seldom did that. I knew I would leave this town one day, I knew I was going to take the Trans-Siberian to Vladivostok, but I did not always know why I did what I had just done.

I put on my warm things and tied the scarf tightly round my neck, and together we walked up the main street to Nytorv and forgot that we ought to be home for supper. I held Jesper's hand though I knew he thought he was too big for that, but it was dark out and night time and not many people could see. Only one man turned into an alleyway and we could hear he was drunk and being violently sick down one of the house walls.

At the end of the square was the Court House with the lock-up on the left. We looked in on our way past but there was no one there, and then we crossed over Gammeltorv to the Aftenstjernen on the opposite side. The old inn lay at a crossroads where one way wound down to Frydenstrand health resort which was closed for the season, and another led straight past the Home for Retired Artisans. Forty years later my father would end his days there.

We saw Lucifer standing by the inn door, he was restless, tossing his head and snorting, and there were shadows playing and golden light in the windows and golden light on the cobblestones from the street lamps above, and when we came to a point midway between two of them we threw shadows in both directions. Jesper had clogs on so you could hear us coming from a long way off. But we were not the only ones. Suddenly there was shouting and hoofbeats and wheels on the cobbles. We turned round and saw a big landau rolling up Danmarksgade, it sounded loud between the houses where the road was narrow and doors flew open, people came out and some boys began to run after the black carriage with its silver embellishments. They hallooed and yelled:

"Throw us some coins, Baron!"

It was Baron Biegler, squire of Bangsbo, in his heavy sheepskin furs, he slapped the door and yelled:

"Faster, coachman! I'm parched as flaming hell!" The coachman whipped up the two horses, they strained against their harness and each would have run to the side if they had not been yoked together. The carriage swung across the square and as it went by the baron leaned out and threw a handful of coins through the night, they sparkled in the light from the street lamps and jingled on the cobblestones before us, rolled to right and left and came to rest in the cracks between the cobbles, but we did not bend to pick them up. We were strictly forbidden to touch that money. It was blood money, my father said. I had no idea whose blood it came from, but they were shinier coins than any I had seen, and Jesper put his hands to his sides and shouted after the carriage:

"Keep your blood money, Baron! You'll soon be dead, anyway!"

I threw myself at him and pulled at his coat:

"What are you saying! You mustn't say such things," I hissed at him as loud as I dared, and one of the boys came up close to us, dropped to his knees and started to pick up coins.

"Get away with you, everyone knows he's got a disease that's killing him."

"But he *is* the baron, isn't he?"

"A circus baron, a pantomime baron, an upstart and a bloody brute!" Jesper yelled with words that were not his own, that he had learned heaven knows where, and the baron's face loomed out of the carriage window like a white mask with three empty black holes before the horses turned in beside the Aftenstjernen and stopped.

"What's he going there for?" said Jesper, "surely he's got plenty to drink at home with all those fine bottles of his."

"Perhaps he's lonely," I said.

"He's a blockhead," said Jesper. "Come on."

He walked across the square as soon as the baron had gone into the inn, the boys had vanished with all the money and we were alone again. I followed him quietly, feeling uneasy.

"Maybe we should go home now," I said, "we should have been in for supper long ago."

"Grandfather is in there, I want to see him. He is my grandfather, and yours too," he said without turning round and then he was at the windows peering in. He was yellow in the face and black down his back His face turned yellow and his back was all black and the coachman sat on the driver's seat staring at the wall and not even looking at Lucifer who was still more restless now with the two new horses beside him.

"I'm going home!" I called.

"All right, then," said Jesper to the windowpane, "I can see quite well alone." I could barely hear him, his black back had diminished until it was just a streak against the golden light, did he really want to be alone? I could not believe it, he was older than me, he was going to die first, and if *he* didn't know that, *I* had known it for ages, and was it really wintertime? I remember it all as winter, the early dark and the empty streets and the cold that crept in under my coat and up my back, and I turned and walked across the square thinking of my mother who was sure to be standing in the doorway by now waiting. Then I stopped, turned round again and ran up to Jesper. I pressed my nose to the glass and felt him against my shoulder.

"I knew you'd come back," he said, laughing softly, and I do not know if I thought it then or several years later, I definitely can't have been more than twelve and Jesper was fourteen, but the cold down my back was unbearable, and I knew I would not always have to stand outside in the dark looking in at the light. I was shivering all over and I felt a sudden urge to smash the window in front of me or get away as fast as possible. But I stayed there with my shoulder against Jesper.

One of the windows was ajar and heat came flooding

out with the light and we saw the baron leaning against the bar-room counter. He cleared a place for himself with one hand so the glasses toppled and rolled over the edge and broke on the floor.

"To hell with it, I'm paying!" he yelled, turning round with a brimming glass in his hand and being *The Baron*.

"This town is full of peasant farmers. Skål, peasants!"

There were no farmers there apart from Grandfather. I knew who they all were. Most of them worked at the shipyard, some were fishermen and a few were artisans like my father. He knew them and met them sometimes, and every summer they went on an excursion to the west coast with the retired workers, but he never went to the Aftenstjernen at night.

The baron was annoyed and raised his glass again.

"Drink up then, for Christ's sake, peasants! Do I have to pay for you?"

Grandfather sat at a table near the door. I could only see his hand holding a glass, but I knew it well and we heard the scraping of chairs and table when he got to his feet and said:

"I pay my own way and I don't drink with any toy baron," and took two steps forward so that his whole body came in sight. He wore his flat-brimmed hat, he was tall and thin without his coat and not quite steady as he walked between the tables towards the counter where the baron was standing.

"I'm going in," said Jesper.

"They're going to fight."

"Exactly."

36

"But you're not allowed to, you're not old enough."

"I'm fourteen, that's more than enough," he said and I looked in again and saw Grandfather and Baron Biegler standing close together each with a glass in his hand. They both had beards that almost touched and Grandfather's hat cast a shadow over the baron's face and his own so you could not see where one ended and the other began. The baron hit out with his arm to protect himself and the spirits in his glass splashed down Grandfather's dark suit and then Grandfather took hold of the sheepskin and started to shake and tug.

"Now they're off," I said.

"I'm going in then," said Jesper. And he went, straight past the coachman who still sat there as stiffly as before, in through the double doors and only when I could see him inside from my place at the window did I hurry after him.

The heat hit me. It came from the four-storeyed stove in the corner and from all the bodies sitting and standing round the tables, and the way across to the counter was clear like the walkway through a byre where the cows stood steaming on each side. I could just glimpse Jesper in there, he clung on to the baron's back with his arm hard around his neck, and the baron kicked backwards with his iron-tipped heel, but there was so much smoke and steam in there it was difficult to see much else, and for a moment I was certain it *was* a byre I had walked into.

A voice that brought everything to a halt cut through the smoke.

"Where did that lass come from? Get her out of here!"

I had seen but not realised that only men were in there, and now I saw all the faces and eyes staring at me. Dead silence fell. Grandfather turned round slowly. He was still holding his glass. It looked ridiculous, and he seemed to realise that because he looked down at the glass and was about to put it on a table, but instead he took a gulp and only then put it down. Now it was empty. He stared at Jesper hanging round the baron's neck, and he put his hand to his hat and shook his head and turned right round, followed the direction of the eyes around him and caught sight of me standing in front of the door in my coat. It was bright blue and quite visible, and I was sure he had seen it many times before. But all the same he peered at it vaguely, took his hat right off and bent forward before he drew a breath and roared:

"What the hell is this? Alcohol Concern, is it?!" Rough laughter came rolling from the counter in a wave towards the door, it hit me in the face and I burned with shame and the heat from the stove after the cold outside.

"It is *you* who should be ashamed!" I shouted though he had not said anything about *me* being ashamed of myself, but there was nothing but shame in there now. The door behind me burst open, a cold draught swept up my back as the laughter rolled backwards to the counter. A hand clamped down on my shoulder. It hurt and I did not need to look round to know who had arrived.

"Go outside and wait till I come," said my father. His voice was gentle, almost kind and his hand was hard. I did not want to go out. It was cold outside and warm inside, but also filled with huge staring eyes, so I turned, took two steps and stopped in the doorway.

The sound of a crash came from the other end of the room. Jesper had landed on the floor, he kicked and floundered and the baron snarled:

"Miserable peasant boy! Are you mad?"

"I'm no peasant, I am a proletarian!" shouted Jesper. Laughter rose again. The regulars at the Aftenstjernen had not had such entertainment since New Year's Eve, but Jesper had read Nexø's books and Pelle the Conqueror was his latest hero. He was going to be an industrial worker and a shop steward and lead his comrades towards the red sun and the New Human Being. Not a brick or a haystack would be left of the old world, and certainly no baron who was generally so drunk when he was going out to hunt in his forests that he could not even walk across his yard without falling on his back, and then crawled on all fours through horse dung and straw to his dovecote, let the pigeons out and shot them instead. And that's no lie.

My father walked through the inn he knew so well with a different light through the windows, now I could see his back and Jesper in there. Jesper was kneeling and brushing dust off his jacket and trousers with one hand while he fended the baron off with the other, and then he looked up and stiffened. He took a big breath and got cautiously to his feet, he did not take his eyes off my father's and he was biting his lip. Now no one spoke. I closed my eyes and waited for the sound that was about to come, for my father's dark voice and his hands that could crush whatever he liked, I had seen that in the workshop when he could not make something work, but it was Grandfather who said:

"Well, if it isn't our joiner-master master-joiner. The prodigal son of agriculture, the good shepherd of saw-dust. What's he doing out so late with practically the whole of his family? Isn't it warm enough at home?"

My father stopped short in the middle of the floor.

"Jesper, just you come with me," he said in a low voice, and Jesper went on looking him straight in the face and began to walk.

"Hey, hey, what's the hurry. Now we're all here together we may as well have a drink, surely? Hee, hee. You stay here, Jesper." Grandfather opened his hand and stretched it out. Jesper stopped, but he did not turn round, and it was I who called:

"He's coming with us!"

My father turned in a flash.

"Be quiet, girl!" he said sharply and the shame was there again and the big eyes, but Jesper was frightened, only I saw that. He stood stiffly between Grandfather and my father, one tall and thin, sneering scornfully in his beard, the other with a bulge at the top of his back almost like a hump and his jaws pressed hard together. No one looked at the baron any more. He did not like that, he put his hands to his sides and said in a voice full of sand and gravel:

"What a damfool family drama! Bloody hell, do we have to listen to this!" He spat on the floor and Grand-father turned and punched him right in the stomach, the baron's back struck the counter and he slid down and came to rest on the floor with his furs like a garland around him. Grandfather picked up the baron's glass and downed it in one gulp.

"Now, Master Joiner," he said, and I could not understand what was wrong with my father's name that it could not be spoken aloud, his name was Magnus, Grandfather knew that well enough, but his voice sounded different from the one I was used to: "Why don't you just go home if you won't drink with your own father? You were never like the others, were you? You have never known why, born in pain and begotten in more than pain, a thorn in the flesh from the start. Go home to your warm house and leave the boy with me."

He rocked backwards and forwards on his heels, but each word rang clear and everyone in the Aftenstjernen sat still and listened, and when he had finished they all looked at my father. He had nothing to say, he just stared straight ahead of him with clenched fists, his back rounder than ever. I tried to catch Jesper's eye and managed it. I beckoned him to me, held his eyes with mine and whispered:

"Come on, come." He came to himself and began walking, and then he did something no one had expected. He went right up to my father and put his arms round him and gave him a hug. One man laughed, but there was no shame in it this time, he just laughed and started to clap and a moment later everyone joined in. They laughed and clapped and stamped their feet on the floor. My father straightened his back and smiled cautiously, he

41

nodded to someone he knew, took hold of us both by the shoulder and led us towards the door. There Jesper turned on his heel, pointed at the baron and shouted:

"You're doomed!" The laughter rose again and my father seized Jesper by the collar and lifted him over the threshold, but I knew he was not angry any more.

Before I closed the door behind us I saw Grandfather standing alone with the baron's empty glass in his hand, and for a moment it occurred to me that he thought Jesper had meant *him*.

4

What my mother was good at was telling stories. And singing songs. She was a composer of hymns. Her maiden name was Aaen, she came from Bangsbostrand, due south of the town where we lived. There they were almost all fishermen and every one of them was a Christian, and the Aaens were more Christian than the rest. The members of that family always spoke in a much more educated manner and did not use the Vendelbo dialect as did most people in the district who were not incomers, and they were so Christian that when they started a co-operative it was called The Co-operative Society of Our Lord. I think it still exists. Those who did not belong to the Co-op faced the winter with foreboding, and when the fishing failed they stood at the door of Our Lord and begged to be let in, but by then it was too late. That was how they learned their lesson.

I do not know why they felt themselves superior. They had no reason to. Possibly it was because the family possessed a camera. A wealthy German had left it behind in payment for the loan of a boat when he stayed as a tourist one summer and rented a house down by the beach. His name was Eisenkopf.

There are a lot of photographs from that time, one of them shows my maternal aunts on their way up

Søndergade from Møllerhuset Allé, they are wearing big hats and long dresses with all kinds of trimming and stuff, and they do not look like fisherman's daughters. But that's what they were. Anyway I am sure my mother felt she had married beneath her although my father came from Vrangbæk which is no small farm even today. One of my uncles became sexton of Bangsbostrand church and had white skin and soft hands, but his son Kurt works at the shipyard and Aunt Else was never anything but a fisherman's wife and in the end a fisherman's widow when her husband Preben went down with the *Lise-Lotte* north of Skagen one moonless January night. She only just scraped through the following years with support from the congregation.

My mother had a piano that my father had bought and adapted when the old cinema closed down. It still had the sound of silent films and when she played it and sang it was a mixture of Chaplin and Christianity that seemed improper to me, but I don't think she thought of it like that. She sat on the stool and felt her way over the keys and wrote down sentences and words in big brown books. The piano remained with her for the rest of her life, and when she finally moved to a rest home the piano went too. Even though she lived in another world most of the time she could sit down and play and sing and suddenly stop and say:

"Oh, wasn't that a really lovely hymn. I wonder who wrote it?" And then after a few minutes she would smile and put her hand to her face and whisper to herself:

"But of course, I did!" Then she laughed with a pride I

felt was equally improper. Many people thought she was probably as good as Kingo, the renowned Danish seventeenth-century hymn-writer, but she never sent her hymns out anywhere and only the family and friends in the congregation were allowed to hear them.

Personally I could not stand them.

Jesper was fond of her. He remembered her birthday and called her Lillemor because she was so short, and he was not above teasing her mercilessly about it. Then she would hit him with the dishcloth, give up and start to blush and giggle. If I tried anything like that there would be a slap and no laughing.

My mother told us about Sara in the woods and about the Man from Danzig. She sat on a chair by the door and Jesper and I lay in our beds as the man sailed through the room in his ship more than a hundred years before from what was Germany, a solitary helmsman with sting-ing eyes and the wind in his hair, with a cargo for Norway, and the weather was dark and stormy and the visibility poor. He was aiming to sail close to the island of Læsø between Sweden and Denmark and he looked out for lighthouses and steered by any he could see. Suddenly lights were everywhere. He tugged at the tiller and steered to starboard, realised that was wrong and turned to port again, and the lights came from all sides and then he hit bottom with a crash and stuck fast, then started to take in water. In the dark he heard the roaring of breakers and splashing of oars and the thumping of small boats against the hull, and he thanked his Lord he was saved. But the men who climbed aboard didn't even look his way, they glided across the deck towards the hatches, and in no time his whole cargo had vanished over the rail and the men had gone with it. Without the cargo the ship lifted off the reef and floated out into deeper water, and there it sank quietly until it vanished with the man from Danzig still on board, and my mother began to whisper:

"The spit where he went aground is known as the Man from Danzig to this day."

"Bloody hell, right scum, they were," said Jesper after my mother had gone. It was all dark inside and dark outside, an endless January darkness, but I knew from the direction of his voice that he was sitting up in bed, and he meant the men from Læsø who had lighted lanterns to trick the man from Danzig into going aground so they could plunder the cargo. He was right, of course, and I was exasperated because what I dreamed of at night was the Man from Danzig at the bottom of the sea amidst kelp and seawrack with eyes like burning charcoal and long wavy fingers that stretched out to grab me. But I realised that was because of the way my mother told the story, and I wondered for a long time whether she felt sorry for him at all. Perhaps she had relations on Læsø, or perhaps they were so poor there they felt they had to be wreckers. That was something else to wonder about.

That winter everything turns into ice. There is snow in the streets, snow on the fields and the ice lies shining on the frozen sea right out to the small islands called

Hirsholmene when the wind blows low from the north and sweeps aside everything in its way. It has been cold before, but not so cold as this, and no one has seen this much snow for twenty years. Some say it was once possible to walk dryshod to Sweden and back again, but that must have been long ago, and I think the cold has something to do with Grandfather, that it comes seeping in after someone has hanged themselves or taken their life in some other way, and it seems to happen particularly in a town where such a death has occurred. But my father says it is cold all over Denmark, and that is really too much to blame Grandfather for, so the theory does not hold water, even though Jesper rather liked it.

I'm in the classroom looking out of the window at the wind tearing at the trees and I hear it howling around the corner of the school. The old windows are not windproof, there is a fiendish draught along the wall and those of us sitting in the window row have put on all our outdoor clothes. Marianne whose desk is in front of me has a big red scarf round her neck, her breath issues like frosty vapour while those along the opposite wall near the stove take off almost all their clothes and smirk sweetly and meanly at us on the outer row. In particular that slob Lone, the headmaster's daughter. She is pretty. She wears a newly-ironed dress every day, has fair curls and gets good marks. So do I. Get good marks. The two of us are far ahead of the others. She is because she gets everything free, I am because I work hard. If I am ever to get away from this place and right to the other end of the world, I need good marks. First the middle school and after that the sixth form, then my door will open. My mother thinks I am good at learning and sometimes even tells me so, but she despairs of Jesper, who takes things more lightly because he's going to be a worker in the ship-yard and a socialist and train himself for opposition. If you are going to be an activist you do not need to do lessons. That's the first commandment, thinks Jesper, and believes he's well on the way. So he is in trouble at school and gets scolded at home.

On the way home from school I walk right behind Lone and mimic the way she moves. She minces along. I go on doing that as long as it is fun, and Lone never once looks back. She lives in a big house in Rosevej almost at Frydenstrand. I don't go as far as that, but in the same direction. We never walk together. Lone is upper class and must not be seen in my company. The feeling is mutual. But as I'm about to turn up Asylgade she does turn round. She stares at me with eyes full of hate, takes hold of her scarf and wrenches it round so the knot is at her nape and hitches it up until it's really tight, sticks out her tongue and squints at me. At once I start to run, hit her with my shoulder and knock her backwards into a snowdrift. I give her a thorough ducking. She may be the headmaster's daughter, but no one makes game of me. No one.

There are several big houses in Rosevej. When my mother goes out for a walk that is where she often goes, down the road and back again, and I know what she is thinking. She's thinking what a good life the people there enjoy. They must be happy. To live so well. Once we went out together, my day was aimless anyway, nothing but empty hours one after the other until darkness fell and my body in the way everywhere. We walked past one of the houses and looked into the garden. It was a big garden, and in the middle of the lawn a young girl sat in a wheelchair. It was summer time then, her face was in shadow and she wore a red dress with a ray of sunshine over her chest. My mother turned and said:

"There, think of that. Better to be poor and able to walk than rich in a wheelchair."

But she is talking to herself. What I see is a girl without a face in a red dress, often at night when I'm asleep, and at first there is just darkness and then the red comes and spreads until it fills everything and I have to wake up or explode, but I do not dream of being rich. My mother does that, somewhere behind the place the hymns come from.

"Why couldn't he at least have given us a house," she says when we hear Grandfather has not left us anything. The Aftenstjernen had taken its share and the house we live in is not our own but belongs to the Baptist church next door. My father is the janitor there. The only thing we own is the carpenter's shop, and though it may be true that my father is the best joiner in town he is not the best at making money. He has so many acquaintances, the town is too small for a professional. They come in from Danmarksgade, across the yard where the cobblestones are slippery with ice and into the golden light from the lamp above the workbench, throw shadows over the sawdust and wood shavings and the piles of mouldings along the walls. They stand fingering well-used yellow-brown tools, keeping at a safe distance from the bandsaw in the middle of the floor, chatting about the times that have never been worse, and my father nods and asks after someone's mother and has she recovered from breaking her thigh and is the son better now? It's not often that things are better, and my father nods again, he knows how it is. When they have gone away they leave a dusty emptiness behind them, the air is stuffy and lifeless like the bottom of a purse, and my father gets to work on the cupboard or the chest and shapes up and remakes and polishes and rubs until the surfaces shine with the glow that is at the heart of all wood, shining without any varnish and with handles of finely carved bone. After a few days they come to fetch it, and then the piece stands there in the centre of the floor as good as new, better than new, and I have searched for the word year after year, looked it up in books and thought and pondered and found *substance*. They bring a wreck and leave with *substance*, and they see it and look dumbfounded and praise my father until his ears flame. When they have gone he has charged them the same amount as last year and the year before that and the year before that again.

In the evenings he sits at the living-room table gazing at the bills with his pencil in his right hand and the rationed cigar in his left. There is rent for the Baptists and coke for the stove and gas for the kitchen range and a new blade for the saw. There is Jesper to be confirmed.

Jesper doesn't want to be, but he must. He will have his first suit and the whole family will be invited. My father sits writing down numbers on paper, he only takes every other pull at his cigar. He should have had a house built of wood that would smell like the workshop from floor to ceiling and not of mould as it does here after the autumn and driving rain on the outer walls. Here everything is brickwork and cement. The water seeps in through the cracks and spreads in damp flowers through the wallpaper so it peels off and the kitchen floor is icy to the feet even in summer with the sun shining in. There is no glow in bricks. In Siberia the houses are built of timber that gives off the good smell of tar and warmth in summer, and when the long winter sets in the glow stays in the logs and never fades. The wood contracts and waits and stretches out when spring comes and drinks in the wind and the sun.

When no one is listening my father grinds his teeth. But I listen all the same. I show him books with pictures of Siberia and the houses there, and he slowly holds it at a long-sighted distance and after a while he says:

"That's a good piece of craftsmanship. But it is cold outside, terribly cold."

I do like it when summer comes with warm wind inside my dress on my bare thighs, but I don't think the cold will bother me. They have different clothes in Siberia that I can learn to wear instead of now when I have only my thin coat against the wind that comes in from the sea between Denmark and Sweden and blows straight through everything. They have caps made of wolfskin and big jackets and fur-lined boots, and lots of the people who live there look like Eskimos. I might pass as one of them if I cut my hair short. And besides I shall sit in the train and look out of the window and talk to people, and they will tell me what their lives are like and what their thoughts are and ask me why I have come all the long way from Denmark. Then I will answer them:

"I have read about you in a book." And then we'll drink hot tea from the samovar and be quiet together just looking.

I brush the snow off the front of my coat and see Lone disappearing with her school bag under her arm and her cap in her hand. She isn't mincing now, and then I still don't go up our road, but down the main street until I get to the gateway and the rear courtyard where the workshop is. I walk through the gateway and see my father coming out of the door of the workshop with his coat on. I wait until he has locked up before I say hallo, and he comes up to me and brushes snow off my back and looks at my face that has a scratch on one cheek.

"Have you been fighting?" he says.

"Yes. With Lone."

"Why?"

"Grandfather," I say, and demonstrate what she did, turning my scarf back to front and pulling it until it's tight, and then he says:

"Are they talking about it at school?"

I nod, and he tightens his lips and walks out through the gateway and locks that too and won't be going back today.

"Where are we going?" I ask.

"*We* aren't going anywhere. *I* am going to the savings bank."

"What are we, I mean what are *you* going there for?"

"To borrow money. You can come along if you stay behind and wait nice and quietly."

He goes in through the heavy door, and I wait nice and quietly till he comes out again only a quarter of an hour later. He stays there on the steps beside me saying nothing before I look up into his face, and then he says very very softly:

"That didn't go too well."

I don't know what to make of this.

"That's a shame," I say a bit too lightly, running down the steps and starting to walk off. But he does not follow. He stands there with his hands in his coat pockets staring straight at the wall on the other side of the street, and when I speak to him he doesn't answer. He runs his hand down his chin and turns.

"Wait here," he says and goes inside again.

This time he's gone half an hour. It's too cold to stand still so long. I jump around and walk up and down the street looking into the windows and thinking what I could have bought if I'd had any money. But it's not good to borrow money, and it was my father who said that. "If you're broke they'll tear the ears off you if you've borrowed money," he'll say.

His ears are red when he comes out and I think they may have tried to tear them off in there, but I don't say that, I say:

"Did it go better this time?"

He takes out a cigar and lights it, it's the last but one, and he takes a long drag before replying:

"You could say that. They've lent me money, but I've pledged the workshop as security."

5

The missionaries travel all over the world, to the benighted regions, to Tasmania and the negroes in Africa and further to the Far East. They spread God's grain among those who wander through barren valleys, and have to suffer bitter hardship. Sometimes they are slain, their heads struck off, or thrown to the lions or buried in the earth with only their heads showing so the ants can slowly devour them. But they do not give up, they have God's hand of authority at their backs. Each year new ones start out from the mission centres and every week we get the missionary journals through the post. Sometimes I read them if there's nothing else, but my mother really studies them. She shows me the journals with pictures of fair-haired women and men who stand tall beneath distant stars, and she says:

"Perhaps you can be a missionary," because she knows I want to travel and to her that is the only route. But I don't want to be eaten by ants and I don't want to be a missionary. I am too short, my hair is dark and I would much rather sit still keeping quiet and listening to the people I meet telling *me* about themselves.

But when the journals arrive I'm the first to look through the contents to see if anyone has gone to Siberia. They never have, but I can't be sure. One day my road is suddenly blocked and the train trapped in a wall of bibles. There it stands with steam from the valves swirling out on both sides groaning without hope over silent steppes.

My mother sits by the window in the evenings, there is a lamp between her chair and my father's, and she reads and smiles with delight over each soul that is saved, and when someone in the Congo has perished from malaria, she puts down the magazine on her lap and sniffles:

"Dear oh dear, the poor soul!" And then she goes to the piano and plays and sings one of her own hymns, and her high-pitched voice fills the room until the walls crack. It seems as if she will never stop, my father rustles his newspaper, but that doesn't help and he puts it down and says:

"For God's sake stop it, Marie!" The flood of sound breaks off and she bows her head and looks down at the keys.

"Oh, Magnus," she whispers. My father repents all over, but he cannot stand it. I can't either. I stand at the door not knowing whether to go or stay, and yet *he* is the one who chose *her*. I don't understand it, they never touch each other, but she has told us about the young man with his powerful arms and a back bent over at the top like a hump. He came cycling along every morning in rain or shine when she was on her way to Søndergaden to stand behind the counter in Jensens Tailors and Dressmakers. He passed her at the crossroads where Vrangbækvej meets Møllehuset allé, and he never said a word, just cycled past and came back and cycled past

56

again, and she tried to look straight down at the road in front of her. But he did not give up. He did tricks on the bicycle to attract her attention. He stood with one foot on the pedal and the other straight out like you see on old circus posters, he hung from the side with his right leg under the bar, he *stood* up on the seat with his hands on the handlebars and he *lay* over the seat with his knees on the luggage carrier, and in that position he let go of the handlebars and sailed imperiously by. He did all this with a perfectly serious expression, and at last she could not help herself and began to laugh. Then he smiled cautiously, pleased. He was twenty, one year younger than her, and too young to get married. But he applied to the King for permission, for he could not wait.

"Christian X, King of Denmark and Iceland, makes it known that Magnus Mogensen, carpenter's apprentice, born 13.3.1889 at Vrangbæk, is hereby given leave to manage his own interests and property before attaining his majority and is permitted to marry shop assistant Marie Aaen, born 25.5.1888 at Bangsbostrand," runs the document he received. It is in my possession now. It is kept in a black box with his obituary notice, and when I think back and try to see him clearly, I more often remember the young man on the bicycle whom I never saw, hanging over the handlebars with a straight and serious face, than the man who was my father when I was young, or the retired joiner at the Artisans' Retirement Home at Kløvervej 4.

In the wet light of a July morning Jesper and I stood at

the very end of the breakwater watching the boat from Læsø come in between the lighthouses and make fast where the old corn silo divided the harbour into two. There had been wind and rain for several days and now it was Sunday and sunny. It was chilly so early in the day and wet on the concrete and the air was damp and still. But big breakers rolled in from the sea and the boat from Læsø rose high between the lighthouses and listed on the inner side until it settled into the harbour basin. I was glad I was not on board, I would have felt queasy and leaned over the rail to vomit into the green water.

Far out to sea lay a blanket of fog and only the tops of the masts could be seen like pins in a pin-cushion where the fishing boats were making for home in convoy after days of hard weather on the banks north of Skagen. Jesper would have liked to stay and see them coming in too, they were quite a sight when they cut through the fog and out into the sudden sunshine. But my father was on board the boat from Læsø, and that was why we were up so early even though it was the middle of the summer holidays. We walked in along the arm of the breakwater to the wharfs at the fishing-boat harbour and the ferry harbour and it was warm inside our wellingtons and cold from the knees up, I felt the gooseflesh spreading and it was a feeling I liked.

We walked fast to get there before the gangway was lowered. We had expected to see him from the breakwater, but my father was not one for standing out on deck to wave to us and be seen by everyone, and he made no exception this time. But there weren't many people in the harbour now. I only saw Hobo-Hans who had slept in a boathouse and two fishermen squatting on a wharf by their boat mending nets, chatting and smoking cigars. The smoke spiralled up into the blue and their voices carried a long way in the early air. We heard them clearly over the water between the projecting piers and they spoke a Vendelbo dialect so old it sounded like English if I did not listen carefully, and I narrowed my eyes as I walked and imagined I was in a dream in a book in another country on the other side of the sea. That went on for a while and then it was over. I hurried over the concrete paving and Jesper jumped from boulder to boulder in the water on the inner side of the breakwater, and it was deep there, for big boats sailed in every day, and if Jesper fell in he might drown.

"Stop doing that," I said, "you'd better come up here. We must hurry, or we won't make it."

"This is quick enough," said Jesper, "I'm almost flying," he shouted and took off on a long leap between two boulders that stuck up high, and he jumped, but one boot got stuck in a lump of tar and stayed there, and he did really fly, and landed head first in the murky water.

It looked odd, one foot in a boot, one foot in a sock, and they hung for a moment before they vanished and a wave rolled in and closed over them and a big bubble leaped out and burst in the mirrored water. And then there was silence.

Complete silence. The fishermen were not talking any longer, they just squatted there looking into the air and the gulls flew without a sound as if they were behind blue-coloured glass and the boat from Læsø had stopped its engine. The silence grew and pressed against my chest and squeezed up the air I had in my lungs until it was in my throat and I had to open my mouth:

"JESPER!"

I climbed down from the concrete paving above the boulders as fast as I could, panting like a dog with no control over my breath or my body, a pump worked in my chest and I couldn't possibly shut my mouth. When I got right down I tore the boot out of the lump of tar and waved it in the air hoping Jesper would come up and get it. But he was gone. I lay down on the outermost boulder and stared into the water and just by my face a hand stretched up with long waving fingers and tried to catch me. It was the Man from Danzig. I gave a start and began panting again, my throat felt sore. I turned round and turned back again and looked down into the water. The hand was still there. Now it was clenched.

"JESPER!" I hurled the boot aside and threw myself forwards. The boulders struck my knees and chest, and it hurt, my chest had developed during the past year and I was soft where I used to be hard. I stretched right out and squeezed my thighs round the last boulder with a clutch that could crush it to powder, and it scraped me back where I was softest. Then I breathed in and plunged my head and upper body into the water. At first my eyes were closed and then they were open, and then I could see his face. It was green with staring eyes and lips pressed together in a thin line. I didn't know if he could see me, but I thought he might and I could not under-

60

stand why he didn't open his hand. It was clenched hard and I had to use both mine to get a good enough grip. I was stronger than any girl I knew, and I pulled. First my head came up and then Jesper's head with his lips pressed together and eyes like marbles. I drew in air, still holding on to him with both hands and screaming as loud as I could:

"BREATHE!" and then his mouth slowly relaxed and he gave a whistling sound that would never stop, and from being stiff he turned completely floppy and finally he closed his eyes.

"I thought you were an angel," he mumbled.

"Angels have fair hair. Besides, they don't exist."

"Mine do, and they have dark hair."

"I thought you were the Man from Danzig," I said. Then he started to laugh and cough, and I pulled him right in till he could get hold of something and crawl ashore by himself. He kneeled down and vomited salt water and breakfast, I held his forehead, and when he was done I hugged the whole of him and started to cry.

"I thought you were the Man from Danzig. I couldn't recognise you." I felt him smile against my shoulder, he was wet through and cold, and warm too, where the sun could reach.

"I looked for him, and I looked for his boat, but there was only seaweed down there, so I wanted to get up again. But I couldn't, the boot was too heavy with all the water in it, and I couldn't get it off. So I just stood there." He embraced me with both arms, shaking so my body trembled, and then I felt shy and stood up.

61

"Thanks, Sistermine," he said.

He emptied the water out of his boot, put both of them on and crawled up on the concrete. Then we started to walk along together. With every other step Jesper took a ripping noise came from the boot with the lump of tar, and I heard the fishermen talking on the wharf and the gulls from all directions and banging sounds from the Læsø boat where the gangway was being lowered and pulled on to the quay.

"Maybe we'll make it after all," said Jesper, speeding up until he almost ran, and I thought how fast it all goes, we had been far away and now we were back and the world had moved on a millimeter.

When we came out of the shadows behind the corn silo the first passengers had already come ashore. They were farmers from Læsø coming to do business and have a beer and visit friends. They were dressed in their best and in their hands they carried cardboard boxes tied with string which might have had eggs in them or home-baked cakes for relatives, but no one had turned up to meet the boat except Jesper and me, and that had been a near thing.

We stopped beside the gangway and the people standing there turned to stare at us. Water ran from hair and clothes and formed puddles around our boots. I ran my hand over my hair that was plastered to my head and had lost its curls and the farmers exchanged looks and started to walk up into town.

My father came ashore last as he usually did. I didn't know why, but thought it had something to do with his back, that he wanted people to see him face first and not walk behind him speculating over the reasons for his being as he was.

Not until he was in the middle of the gangway did he raise his eyes and look at us. He had been on Læsø for several days to see whether we should move over there, if there was any market for a joiner. He still had the money he had borrowed from the bank and could start up with that. I saw in his face that things had not gone well, and the sight of us didn't improve matters. He stopped with his hands gripping the rope so hard that the knuckles turned white and his face grew white with anger. Jesper stood tensely beside me, he did not realise what our father saw, and I quickly took two steps forward and asked:

"How did it go, Father?" but he did not look at me and did not reply, just pushed me aside, grabbed Jesper by the collar and said, low and hard:

"Have you seen yourself! Is this the way to come and meet your father?" although I did not look any better, wet from the waist up, with grazes on my knees and my hair hanging in sticky tangles down my back. I loved my father and his crooked back, my father loved Jesper and all his quirky ideas, but his arms were hard and strong as twisted hawsers, and with those he started to shake Jesper who was fifteen years old and newly confirmed, who was going to help him in the workshop before he began his printer's apprenticeship. It wouldn't do, and I knew it and Jesper knew it, only my father didn't know it. Jesper stood with his legs apart and would not be budged. He was strong and brown too, and his dark mop flopped up and down each time my father pulled at his collar, but from his belt down he stood still. Slowly he let his body stiffen and with bowed head he said:

"Stop doing that," and my father replied furiously:

"What was that?"

"I said bloody well stop doing that!" Jesper raised his head. I could see he was on the verge of tears, and with one hard tug he was free.

"You will never do that again," he said, and it was so embarrassing that he looked neither at my father nor me, but past us at the boat from Læsø where a crane was lifting live animals out of the hold and swinging them ashore, pigs and oxen for the slaughterhouse in our town. They made undignified running movements in thin air and I heard their cries and the ripping noise from Jesper's boot as he turned and walked away.

"You're not going anywhere!" my father called after him, but he did not even look back, just walked on at the same speed until he disappeared behind the corn silo on the way up to the church square and Danmarksgade. His thin jacket stuck to his back and I thought, there goes my brother, Jesper the socialist.

Later on I heard that one of the pigs had committed suicide on the quay. It escaped after they had hoisted it from the boat and ran straight for the edge and jumped into the water and there it was crushed between the boat and the wharf until it drowned. It did not even scream.

6

In one room of Lone's house there are books from floor to ceiling. Another is the dining room. They have lunch and dinner there although the kitchen is big and airy and has wide wooden floorboards. Lone has to change for dinner. She has a room she doesn't share with anyone, there are books on shelves in her room and pictures on the walls and blue curtains. From the window she can look out into the garden where there are big trees that throw shadows on warm days. Lone's mother is at home all day. She goes from room to room with a duster in her hand, she changes tablecloths according to colour and straightens pictures and rows of books. She walks in the garden and picks flowers she arranges in vases on the tables. All the vases are blue, the tablecloths are yellow and green. On Sundays she plays the piano in the library and croquet on the grass in the garden with Lone and her brother Hans. Hans is two years younger than Lone and has to wear a sailor suit on Sunday, he is hot and red in the face when he turns and sees me coming through the gate and up the gravel path to the house. He sneers at me. I stop and stand still until Lone has seen me and waves. I've been friends with that slob since May. When the long winter was behind us we started to talk to each other. Maybe it's the books I can borrow from her, maybe I like her, no one else does. Whatever it is, the war between us is over. She never comes to my house, I have been to hers several times, I have waited in the hall between the rooms and heard her mother talk about flowers and colours and how important it is to have clear contrasts.

"Simplicity is the most beautiful style," she says, smiling at me because she thinks I know something about simplicity, but Jesper says I have shocking taste for a girl. I couldn't care less. Once she takes a book from the shelf and reads aloud from Jeppe Aakjær. She holds the book in her left hand and lifts her right arm in the air when she reads.

"Isn't that good," she says with protruding lips, putting the book back in its right place in the alphabet. I nod and say it is good. Lone's mother believes in poetry. Her father, the headmaster, believes in natural science. He talks about the insects and their world. As often as he can spare the time he goes out in the fields with his rucksack and net to catch insects, put pins in them and hang them up in glass and frame on the wall with Latin names underneath.

"You can learn a lot about human beings by studying the insects," he says, "their world is like ours in miniature, they just have a far better distribution of work." There may be clarity and contrasts in Lone's family, but I don't care for insects. Insects scratch and tickle, they creep up under your dress and sting you.

Every time I go through the gate to Lone's house I remember the wheelchair and the girl in the red dress, the shadows and sunbeams among the trees and roses of

Rosevej. I ask about her and tell Lone the dream I had. Lone says the girl was a cousin from Copenhagen on a visit and to get some fresh air. She is dead now, of tuberculosis. Lone went to Copenhagen by boat to attend the funeral. It was terribly sad, everyone wore suits and dresses and her mother had to sit on a chair because she couldn't stand for grief, and there were people all over the churchyard, dark against the green grass; they were all looking the same way rather like you do at the theatre. Lone once went to the Royal Theatre and she often talks about it.

"I cried through most of the priest's address," she says proudly. The girl's name was Irma, she was in the sixth form and was seventeen. I'm thirteen and I feel strong, stronger than Lone and her brother Hans, almost as strong as Jesper. Lone feels it too, I notice by the way she touches me. Hans has called me a peasant girl several times, that's what they're like, he thinks. Their mother follows me with her eyes when I walk about the house. She's afraid I may break something. I have had rickets, but I got over it, I got stronger by fighting, my mother says, almost unfeminine, only the enamel on my teeth was damaged in several places so I have to take good care and brush them often.

They have all Nexø's books in Lone's home, but not because they like him.

"He is a danger to the country," says Lone's father, "he is a Russian communist and a mole who undermines natural respect," but he wants to keep up to date on what the man in the street is reading, so he gets the books sent from Copenhagen. I've come to borrow Martin Andersen Nexø's novel *Ditte Menneskebarn*, because Jesper hasn't read that, and maybe Knud Rasmussen's book about the great sledge journey across Greenland. I want to read them too, but first I'll take them out to Jesper so he has something different to think about wherever he may be. When my father and I went back from the harbour after the Læsø boat, Jesper wasn't at home. My mother had not seen him, but he had been in, because his wet clothes hung over a chair and dripped on the floor. He didn't come home to lunch at twelve o'clock and not to after-noon coffee either. My father went out in the evening saying he was going to Aftenstjernen, but we knew he never went to that place so late.

Lone is disappointed because I only want to borrow books, she keeps hold of my arm longer than necessary and then she goes to fetch them obediently. I don't go in with her, I stand in the shade of a tree and watch Hans and his mother playing croquet on the lawn. There is a quiet clucking sound from the wooden balls. The grass is lush and green.

"You won," says the mother. He puts his hands on his hips and smiles at her patronisingly. Then he drops his mallet on the grass and turns to walk up to the house. She watches his back the whole way, then she turns and looks at me and her eyes are swimming and her neck under the pinned up hairstyle is pathetic, and I am glad Lone comes out with the books under her arm. On top is a book on butterflies as camouflage, and Hans gives her a shove with his shoulder as they pass each other at the glass door. She drops the books on the stone steps, they slip apart and he bends down and says loudly:

"You're not allowed to take them!" I'm there in a second, pick up the books and look him straight in the eye.

"I'm borrowing those," I snarl quietly. I hate his sailor suit and his water-combed hair and I know he knows it. He turns aside without a word. I carry the books openly past their mother and Lone goes with me to the gate and right out on to the road where my cycle leans against the railings. I tie the books firmly to the carrier and half turn to her saying:

"So long," before I spin off down the road to Frydenstrand and feel her eyes on my back.

"Where are you going?" she calls. I just wave without looking back. She is begging, but guilty conscience only troubles me for a few metres.

I cycle along. There are hedges and roses along white-painted fences and suits and dresses in the shadows behind, and then come cornflowers in carpets of blue and violets in clumps and poppies at the edges of fields next to the gravel road. At the end of the road the smell of cornfields and cow manure drifts from the north, and I conjure up the steam off the milk through the air and straight ahead I see the sea glinting between the trees near the public swimming pool. I have the sun in my face when I turn at the crossroads by Frydenstrand house and out on to the coast road where a puff of wind brings the stench of fishmeal from the harbour and factory there.

I cycle with *Ditte* behind me on the carrier and put my hand on her now and then and Lone disappears among the houses and gardens until I've forgotten her existence. Dog roses are in bloom on Tordenskjold's earthworks, they grow and spread a little more every year and the undergrowth hums with honey bees and bumble-bees. When I stand on the pedals I can see the sea above the bushes and the waves sliding in to the beach with white crests in long streaks as far as the eye can reach and further still and all the way north to Skagen.

I cycle on and think of my father in the streets in the evening, he stops and looks around him at each cross-roads, I think of Jesper at the bottom of the harbour basin with clenched hands, the green face that will not breathe, and the pig that drowned without making a sound. Over the sea in the east the weather that has passed lies in a dark line at the far end of the world and it is warm now and a big sky rises like a film of blue over the whole of Denmark and behind it no one knows what there is. Sometimes at night I lie gazing out of the window and up at the sky and force my thoughts through the firmament to see what they meet on the other side, but in spite of what I learn at school, everything dissolves into small pieces and I have to go to sleep or my head starts to ache.

Strandby is north of our town. All the people there are Baptists and fisherfolk, and halfway there I cross the Elling brook. It is deep and green and full of shadows under a bridge across the road, and soon after that another road leads down to the right. It's just a cart track with parallel wheelruts, and I cycle first in one and then in the other, it bumps so much I have to stand on the pedals so as not to get a pain in the bum, and then I look out over mustard fields growing a metre high on each side. A puff of wind and everything moves.

And then the road opens up and the walls of crops turn into clover and marram grass and the road ends in a hollow of sand which makes cycling impossible. I wheel the cycle for a while until it cannot be seen from the cart track and hide it in some undergrowth before I walk on, carrying the books under my arm. I slide down a sand dune and come out on to the white beach. I see Strandby to the north and the breakwater there just above the marram grass and my town to the south with the big roof of Frydenstrand health baths as a landmark and straight out to sea are the islands of Hirsholmene with the finger of the lighthouse pointing at the sky. I take off my shoes and carry them and walk barefoot on the sand the sun has shone on all day; it burns my feet at first and after a few metres that is really nice. There is not far to go. On the inner side of the beach black and white spotted cows stand chewing the cud behind a barbed wire fence and on the sea side there are big piles of seaweed and stranded jellyfish drying and slowly dying in the sunshine.

Jesper built the little shack out of the driftwood that always lies strewn around on the beach after gales, and I used to go out and help him, dragging heavy waterlogged trunks and long planks from the beach and laying them to dry in the sun. We imagined they were the wreckage of boats that had been sunk and cast ashore here. But of course boats are not built of wood any more, and anyway that was just a game we played.

The shack lies between two slanting dune walls and is invisible until you get right up close, it has a turf roof and a view straight out to sea. I walk silently without seeing anyone, it is quite silent and I wonder whether he has gone somewhere else. But there is nowhere else, only Vrangbæk and we go there as seldom as we can. After Grandfather died and Lucifer disappeared there is nothing but coldness in the rooms out there even in summer. We are sent for when it's time to sow potatoes and mow the first hay and have to work hard for no pay, but that is all.

"You'll have to go," says my father and will not come with us even though it is his childhood home. Then Jesper and I cycle out alone, for we have seen them together, Grandmother at Vrangbæk and her only son, and she stands stiffly at the end of the potato rows with a chalk-white face and sees to it that our backs are not straighter than necessary, and Jesper curses into the furrows and says:

"That feudal-remnant of a squire's hag! One day we'll come back with scythes and pitchforks and there'll be many of us, and then!" Just what will happen then he does not enlarge upon, but I can see in his face that it will be grim.

After Grandfather was in his grave and some days had passed, Lucifer rebelled. The two of them had been together every single day, and Grandfather slept in the stable many times and came out early with straw in his hair, harnessed Lucifer to the trap and went to our town and inland to Hjørring and once all the way to Brønderslev to drink at the inns and come home next morning with the sun.

Now no one could get near the horse. He left his oats and hay untouched in the manger, he kicked and lashed out in his stall so the walls were smashed to splinters. Grandmother grew so fed up with it that she decided the horse must be shot, and sent for Uncle Nils. The night before he was going out there with his gun there was such an uproar in the stable that the whole farm sat up in their beds, and when Grandmother went running with a lantern in her hand and her nightdress flapping across the yard, the stable door was broken and Lucifer far down Vrangbækvej. Before she could gather people for a search, Lucifer seemed to have vanished from this world. Perhaps he had gone to join Grandfather. That was some horse!

Jesper and I took off our caps and wished him luck, and not a week passes when we do not look for him when we go out of town on our bikes. When I spin past Aftenstjernen in the evening I always have to look twice at the space outside the door, but there is nothing there except sometimes Baron Biegler's landau. So Lucifer must have gone for ever.

I walk right up to the shack and round to the back and in at the door that isn't a door, but a blanket Jesper has hung in the opening to keep out the sand. He is never there in winter and the gales usually sweep in from the

73

sea, so there is no need for it now, and when I get inside it's suddenly dark after the sunshine outside. I stand still and wait, breathing in the smell of salt and seaweed drying in the sun and sun-scorched tarred poles, there is a strong smell of wood and warmth and my brother Jesper lies on a mattress under the window breathing in and out in all this. He is asleep and I can see him better with each rise of his chest. It is naked, he lies on top of the covers and is naked all over in the faint light from the window where we have hung a little embroidered cloth my mother made. She had embroidered *Jesus lives* on it. It's a joke, Jesper and I do not believe in either Jesus or God, and I stand quite still holding my breath, for I have never seen Jesper like this, not so clearly, not so whole, even though we have shared a room for several years. There are sun-bleached stripes in his black hair and he is sunburned with a pale area only over his hips and his hips shine and I want to turn round and go out, for I can't stand here. But I see everything plainly in the half-darkness now, his clothes on the floor and the fishing rod in the corner and the cut-out picture of Lenin on the wall and a photograph of himself and me in front of Aunt Else's house at Bangsbostrand. I with my round face and mane of hair and he in his shorts, brown as an Arab with a ball under one arm and the other one around me. It seems to me now that we are so small in that picture, but I do remember when it was taken. Remember the sun we are squinting against and my father who is not in it because Aunt Else said "For heaven's sake, Magnus, can't you smile for once," and he

74

would not smile and angrily walked out of the picture. I remember Jesper's arm around my shoulder, still remember it today if I just close my eyes, even though I am sixty years old, and he has been dead for more than half my life.

I walk forward and put the books on the floor beside the mattress and he does not wake up, just breathes evenly so I can feel it on my face. I stay there standing over him, a long time perhaps, and cannot make myself straighten up. My back will not obey, it hurts from my neck down and heat spreads in my hips, and then I start to cry. I cry as quietly as I can, for I am afraid he will get tears on his face, afraid he will wake up and see me looking at him and my chest hurts when I cry and hold it in at the same time. I look at Lenin's shining scalp and the photograph and think of the ball Jesper holds under his arm that was red and the little black dog Aunt Else had then and the shirts Jesper wore that had buttons on the shoulders so his collarbones showed straight and clear on both sides. I fill my head with thoughts till it feels lilac and hot like the glowing iron at the blacksmith's forge while I stand bent over my naked brother weeping because he is beautiful as pictures I have seen in books of men from other times, grown men, and if I could remember why I came out to find him, it would not mean anything now. He is not the same any more, cannot be and his arm around my shoulder will never be the same again.

7

My father works his way downwards. To start with he had the workshop and a little furniture shop he was given in advance on inheritance because he was a thorn in the flesh and had to leave the farm before his majority.

That was an expression we used now. Thorn in the flesh.

"If she doesn't stop soon, I'll get a thorn in the flesh," Jesper said when my mother played the piano and sang for two hours. He held on to his behind where the flesh was plentiful and moaned and groaned and I could really see it, how the thorn went inwards just as sharp as the sting in *Death, where is thy sting,* sharp and painful, and Grandfather had felt them both. But we couldn't understand why he had used that expression at the Aftenstjernen that time and we did not dare to ask and my father never mentioned the event by so much as one word.

Now he was in debt with the workshop as security. I had never seen the furniture shop. Eventually he bought the Lodsgade Dairy and the tiny flat on the floor above. A steep winding staircase linked the floors with a door giving on to the dairy shop at the bottom of the stairs, and the lavatory was in the yard. The flat was much smaller than the house we had rented from the Baptists.

The whole situation seemed uncertain. My mother was to run the dairy and had less time for her piano and hymns. "Praise the Lord. His name be praised," said Jesper. I had to deliver the milk and cream to the customers before school. I asked my father, and he said Rosevej was a part of our milk round. Jesper had finished with middle school and had to get up early and go to the workshop every morning with an apron on right up to Christmas, and after Christmas he was to be a printer's devil at the local newspaper office. He was pleased about that. The typographers had a strong trade union and there were more socialists there than flies around a pig's arsehole, he said.

So we moved from Asylgade one day in September. There were grey clouds driving across the sky and a strong wind, but no rain. We borrowed a horse and cart from Vrangbæk, Uncle Nils arrived early in the morning with a brown gelding pulling the cart. He sat bare-headed on the driver's seat and the wind tore at his hair and the horse's mane and forelock and it looked unkempt and mournful and nothing like Lucifer had been. Uncle Nils was going to help with the carrying, he usually came rolling up when there was something to be done, silent as always, but Grandmother and my father's half-brothers stayed at home at Vrangbæk and the farms where they lived. My mother could have done with some help in the kitchen, but none of the women came, so I was the one who stood wrapping up cups and glasses in newspaper even though I was strong enough to lift most things, apart from the piano.

Through the window I saw all our possessions under the open sky, and the sky was huge and the wind beat against loose ends of tablecloths and curtains, the furniture had shrunk and took up ridiculously little space although the house had always seemed full. It was not easy to grasp, but there was not much more than one load plus an extra trip for the piano.

At Lodsgade the piano had to go on the first floor up the narrow winding staircase, and my father and Uncle Nils and Jesper had several bad moments on the way up. I stood in the gateway watching the veins swell in my father's forehead and Uncle Nils's grey face and Jesper grinning scornfully all the time.

"I can tell you Christianity was at stake on the bends," he said afterwards – "it was only just rescued. On that staircase I heard words a minor should be protected from. Bloody hell," he said, smiling as he spoke, enjoying himself more than he had for a long while. For a moment he had considered letting go and leaving the piano to fall, then we should be free of that grief, but then my mother might get hold of a cheap organ instead, so it wouldn't have been worth the trouble, especially because my father was lowest down and would have had the piano on his head.

We are closer to the harbour now. I hear the throb of the fishing-boat motors and the cranes of the shipyard at evening and drunk men on their way up from the Færgekroen at midnight. Sometimes I hear animals screaming from the slaughterhouse. That cannot be right. I do not think they scream, but I know how they stand packed tightly together in the compounds waiting and scraping their hooves and perhaps that is the sound I hear when I lie in bed and can't get to sleep.

I walk through our new home, from bedroom to living room, counting the steps, everything is cramped, the kitchen at the top of the stairs has two gas rings and one larder cupboard and room for two people if they *stand* without lifting their elbows. From the little window above the bench I look down into the yard. A little girl I don't know is skipping outside the lavatory. I walk downstairs and through the door at the end and out into the shop and along the counter at the back to a door in the opposite wall that leads into a small side room with a window on to the street. This closet is three metres by three. Jesper and I have to share it. My mother is filled with misgiving, she bites her lip, she thinks it isn't right, she wrings her hands and that irritates me. Though I share her misgiving. Jesper hangs up two pictures of ladies above his bed, one of Rosa Luxemburg and one of Greta Garbo, he hopes they will merge into one when he is not looking, when he sleeps and dreams of the new world. I hang a picture of Lucifer over mine. I want white curtains, he wants red ones, like flags, he says. We end up with one of each, so he gets his flag. It looks peculiar. My father blows into his moustache, he thinks it looks daft, but he makes no comment.

Every night I get undressed under the quilt. Jesper carries on as usual, because he has not changed. It makes me transparent and I have to go up the dark stairs in the middle of the night and look at myself in the big mirror and feel my face and my shoulders and chest while he sleeps. I stand there a long time with the small light on, and when I switch it off I can see myself almost without a face, and I think of Irma in her red dress. She stands freezing cold in a big room, she is rubbing her arms. Then I turn the light on and stay there in front of the mirror until I find myself again, and then I go back downstairs and through the shop. The tiles shine dully in the light of the street lamps, the milk bottles are up to their necks in ice-cold water. I rub my shoulders as I walk past them.

"You brood too much," my mother says, as if she's anyone to talk, she walks into closed doors with both hands in her hair and hairpins in her mouth mumbling and her nose gets flattened.

"Dear oh dear," she says. She is lost in thought at the till with her hand in the drawer searching for change, and she just stands there. A customer can rustle notes before her eyes and her pupils do not move. She is transported from this world, with one foot in heaven, one knee on the stool at communion with the taste of wafer in her mouth.

I stand in the living room looking out of the window between two house plants, I have been standing there half an hour, she says.

"What are you looking at?"

I look out of the window as if for the first time. Herlov

Bendiksen – Glazier, reads a sign on the other side of the street. That is not enough for half an hour.

"Nothing," I say.

I have moved up to Middle School. I like it, I like school and I'm old enough to borrow whatever I want from the library, and I do. I read the books that Jesper reads and I read Johannes V. Jensen and Tom Kristensen who drinks too much and is not a nice man, and I read about Madame Curie. The stacks beside my bed are growing. But Lone isn't at school any more. She just stopped coming and I am lonely at the top of the class. It doesn't taste good. I do not ask after her and no one tells us anything, for her father is head of the school. But sometimes when I'm delivering milk in the morning I look in through the glass door, and I have seen her twice. She sits with her back to the door and does not come out.

One morning when I was a little late her father stood waiting on the stone steps, he nodded at me as if I had never been there before. Now I delivered the milk, the only one in town who was not a boy. He gave me a note asking for their delivery to be doubled. Then he nodded again without looking me in the eye and disappeared inside. There was darkness all around him, gone were the insects with their Latin names, the butterflies and ants and their enviable world. I stayed there on the steps feeling autumn had come. My father would be happy about the extra delivery, but I was not. The goods cycle was heavy enough as it was and if there had not been a wheel on each side of the crate carrier in front I would have crashed on to the cobblestones in a sea of milk more than once.

Then I pedal on and feel my calf muscles growing. They should not be that big on a girl, I get comments in gym lessons, but they make me stand firm, and can be useful for many things. For bracing myself in the playground, for kicking out when I swim, I have already won the school championship in the icy cold water behind Sønderhavn, and I get better and better. Two boys got cramp, I helped one of them up, and I picture long walks in Siberia to remote dwellings that must be made ready to resist the long winter before it sets in. There is weight and substance in all things and I am a girl, but I can walk all day long and keep up with everyone and just feel a pleasant faint trembling in my legs in the evening before I go to bed and sleep like a stone. Sometimes Jesper is there too, brown under his wolfskin cap, because he has just come from southern parts and needs to see other things than palm leaves and walls of hard-beaten clay. And I am happy to have him with me.

That is what I think about when I look out of the window, and I think of Ruben in my class who is the best-looking boy in school now that Jesper has left. He kissed me behind the shed in the playground, and it was all right, but when I went to bed it was already forgotten. He is a Jew. He must have been a Jew before too, but it's something new now, no one thought about it then. All I know about Jews is what my mother tells me, and she says they hanged Jesus on the cross and let Barabbas go free. But Jesus was a Jew also, and anyway that's a struggle I want nothing to do with, I think if the Jews hadn't hanged him on that cross someone else would have, to give my mother something to write hymns and songs about, something to sigh over when she looks up at the big picture above the piano of Jesus on the Mount of Olives. He sits under the moon thinking, tormented in his hour of trial. It fills her life, it filled Asylgade and it fills Lodsgade right down to Færgekroen and then there is a bible-free area right out to the breakwater, according to Jesper.

I do not think Ruben would have chosen Barabbas, but he says he is afraid. Afraid because his father is afraid when he hears news from Germany, particularly after what was called Anschluss in the newspapers.

I too hear news from Germany. From Helga in Magdeburg. We began to correspond more than a year ago, the whole class made contact with a class in that town to boost our German lessons, but I think I'm the only one to get further than the first two letters.

We write about our brothers. Walter is a member of the Hitlerjugend, but Helga does not want to join and her father does not dare say anything to either of them. I dare not tell Jesper about that bit. She describes her dog Kantor who howls each time the soldiers march through the streets singing. She tells me about the great river Elbe that runs through the town, so they have a harbour although Magdeburg is an inland town. I already knew that, it is in my geography book. I have studied that carefully. Her classmates who were Jewish have moved away, she writes. I tell her about Lone and about Siberia. I can do that because Helga is so far away. I do not understand, she writes, there are prison camps in Siberia, das habe ich in der Schule gelernt. But Siberia is a big country, and perhaps she has not learned very much, so I forgive her.

We have arranged to meet. We will go by train from our own home towns and get off at the border and recognise each other at first glance and embrace each other at the precise spot where we are bound to see the line that is drawn between Denmark and Germany. But for the time being there's no money, and everything is so uncertain here, she writes. So we shall have to wait.

I put down the last letter and I must look rather dejected. Jesper stands in the doorway, he has to mind the shop while my mother is out on an errand. He looks at me.

"What's up with you?" he says.

"Helga says there are prison camps in Siberia. She's learned about it at school."

"Nazi propaganda," says Jesper.

8

Now the nights are completely black. Only the white crests of the waves to be seen out at sea when it's windy and the flashing lights from boats coming straight over from Sweden and sometimes I see the light from the port-holes of larger ships and then it is reflected in the black water, lonely and yellow. When I lean out of the window of our little room I can just see down the street and out along the harbour and past the breakwater.

Gas has been found underneath the town and in neighbouring areas. Fifty metres down, sixty metres down, there is gas under the sea and it bubbles up as if from thousands of bottles of pop. People go out in boats on Sundays to look, and boreholes are drilled at Bangsbo and near the Frydenstrand Hotel. They are boring on the lawn behind the Seamen's Home and in several gardens in the town. The gas is piped or put into big bottles and used for stoves and cars, for factories, even the Sæby bus has two long gas containers on its roof. They are heavy, from the inside you can see the roof caving in.

In Danmarksgade the flames of the gas lamps flicker. There are two rings high up under the lamps, and the lamplighter pulls them using a long pole with a hook at the end: he pulls one ring to light the lamp, another to put it out. Jesper used to have great fun sneaking after the lamplighter with a similar pole he had made, and when the man in black uniform had pulled one ring and gone on to light the next lamp, Jesper scurried out of the shadows and pulled the opposite ring. They went on like that right up to Nytorv. When the lamplighter had arrived there he always turned to contemplate his work, for he was the lord of light and darkness, and then the whole street might be pitch black.

"Now that was really worthwhile work," says Jesper, "but hell, I haven't time to go on with it now."

And that's true. He puts in long days at the workshop and by evening he is completely worn out, for my father drives him hard. His head buzzes with the screaming of the saw and he is faint from the lack of voices. Jesper likes to talk, likes to tell stories, likes to *listen to* stories, but my father does not say much and works all day long bowed over his bench with his back to Jesper, and that humped back is big and hard . . .

". . . as a rock," says Jesper.

In the evenings he often goes out to meetings of the Spain Committee. The war there is raging in its third year and I feel good when I'm alone in the room, being able to read what I want without comments or just to gaze out of the window and not have to explain what I'm thinking about when I'm thinking of what I call nothing. But still I do miss him. There is not much laughter indoors when Jesper is out.

Lone is dead, but no one says what she died of. It is not mentioned at our dinner table and nobody else I talk to knows. When I deliver the milk to Rosevej there are always lights on in every room, and again when I cycle past in the evening the lights are on. I think they must be on all the time. Nobody waits on the steps when I get there in the morning, but the delivery is back to normal again. That was written on a scrap of paper fixed to the door frame. I sometimes see Hans at the top of the town, but he never even makes faces, just turns his back as if I was the one who had infected Lone with something indescribably terrible. I have not, no one can say that. But I feel miserable. I feel like being ill, really ill, and just lying in bed looking up at the ceiling and making myself go empty. But I am too strong and will not be left in peace. There are customers ringing the bell and bottles clinking and loud voices, there is my mother wringing her hands and asking what she can do, it is not like me, she says, and Jesper comes in and has to go to bed or just *be* there. So I go to school. I work even harder at my lessons, and my marks have never been better. But I don't feel at all triumphant.

Where I live now there is no one to keep me company on the way to school, not many families live in the harbour area, so I have to walk on my own when the milk is delivered and my bike parked in the yard. When I come back along Lodsgade at three o'clock my mother is standing on the steps to the shop, she looks at me and says:

"If you walk along with your nose in the air you'll never make any friends," and says for the first time what I have heard for the rest of my life, that I am stuck up.

But that is not true, I have friends. I have Marianne and Ruben and Pia and others, we go cycling and swimming, but I get queasy if I look at the ground when I walk. I hold my head high and glance sideways over the rooftops.

"What's the weather going to be like?" asks Jesper. He follows my gaze and uses me to forecast the weather.

"Light cloud cover with glimpses of sun," I reply and can't help laughing.

"That's fine," he says, "we could do with some sunshine now. And you could do with tripping the light fantastic. I'm going out tonight, shall we say ten o'clock?"

Ten o'clock is my bedtime, I have to get up early for the milk and I like to go to bed before Jesper comes in and have an hour to read by the light from the street. I'm just fourteen now and he's almost seventeen and we both look more. Everyone says so. I look at him sideways. He's different, narrower in the face, older, but now he's here again.

"Find something to wear," he says.

I go down to the little room at quarter to ten as usual, saying goodnight on the way, and once in the room I go to the wardrobe, search and find the blue dress I wear at Christmas and important birthdays. I mustn't wear it out, it must be saved, my mother says, and it is the only decent thing I have. I brush my hair till it foams around my head and get out my light shoes from under the bed, then sit down with my coat on my lap and wait. A little later he comes down.

"Why do they always want to chat when you haven't

got time, and only then," he says.

I look out of the window while he changes. He notices, maybe for the first time. I feel his eyes on my back, everything goes quiet and then he starts to whistle the International.

All the clothes he owns hang over the chair beside his bed. At regular intervals the chair falls over and all the clothes land on the floor in a heap and stay there. Sometimes for ages.

"You need to have a clear picture of what's in your wardrobe, otherwise it'll be sheer chaos," he says and finds what he is looking for in the heap. He always does this. *My* clothes hang in a neat row in the wardrobe and yet I'm the one who often stands there unable to choose what *I'm* going to wear.

The wrought-iron gates to the yard are closed after nine o'clock and my father keeps the key, although Jesper has told them upstairs he is going out, and with me in tow we cannot go the usual way past the stairs, across the entrance and out into the street. So we go through the dairy shop, and Jesper has the key to *that* door in his pocket.

We get behind the counter and people are walking by in the light on the pavement and it's dark in the shop between the shelves furthest in. We stay in the shadow of the icebox waiting. Jesper has hold of my shoulder. He is a head taller than me, my mother says I won't grow any taller, perhaps she is right. When the street is empty again I walk towards the door, but Jesper bends over the sink where the milk bottles stand in water with only their necks sticking up and takes out a half litre bottle. A ray of light falls through the window, it drips and sparkles, he pulls down the cap and takes a long gulp, like a man in the Sahara.

"God, I was thirsty, skål, Sistermine," he says to the ceiling and takes another gulp.

"That costs twenty-five øre," I say, without knowing why.

"Money's the one thing I've got plenty of, Your Stinginess. I'll soon be upper class on the pay I get from him up there. You'll have to clean my shoes. Here." I take the bottle and drink from it too. It tastes rich and cool and slightly sickly, I would rather have it hot with honey before going to sleep. But I finish what is left and put the bottle behind the counter.

Jesper cautiously unlocks the door. Before he opens it he takes a woollen sock out of his pocket and pushes it into the bell so it won't ring when we go out. He may have done this often before and I imagine a secret life after dark when he walks through shadowy back streets to dim rooms with a password at the door and men with cover names and low voices leaning over tables and behind them faceless women in tight dresses showing most of their breasts, and long legs in net stockings under their dresses and all of them completely different from me. I feel like going in again, letting Jesper vanish alone into the evening and leaving me in peace, for I have to get up early tomorrow. But then I remember he's always sound asleep when I have to go upstairs in the night; that his bed is never empty, but on the contrary seems to fill the small room, and I catch a glimpse of us both in the big plate-glass window of Herlov Bendiksen's, on the way out of a darkened shop. Jesper in the loose coat he bought with his own money and his black hair that has grown long and full of curls, and me with my coat and my beret on top of all the abundant brown. And I become what I see. I see a book in which this is the beginning and no one knows yet what will happen and why we are coming out of a dark shop at this time of night. There are butterflies in my stomach and a weight-less feeling before what is to come.

"Where are we going?"

"You'll see that when you see it."

We went north along Danmarksgade, past the gateway into the back yard where my father's workshop was in a low half-timbered building, and right up to the Løveapotek and the church square. The street lights were lit the whole way, no one had taken up where Jesper had left off.

"The young are workshy nowadays. It's a sad sight," he said. "I haven't got a pole any more, maybe I could climb up." He went over and tried putting his arms round a lamp post and calculating the distance to the top.

"*I* can do that," I said. "Jesper, let me do it."

I ran up to the lamp post and pushed him aside, got hold of it as high as I could and started to pull myself up. I was strong enough, I was a squirrel, my arms could take it and the gloves I had on gave a good grip. At the top I squinted at the flame, pulled the ring, and the flame sank and went out. I leaned my forehead against the post for a moment, I was as hot as if I had a temperature, my head ached, and then I lowered myself down to Jesper. He stood with his hands at his sides, smiling.

"There's hope yet," he said. "The coming generation has seized the torch and extinguished it for a while. "Light over the land, that is what we want," but not at all hours. Well done, Sistermine."

When we had gone a little further up the street I turned round and looked back. In the row of lights there was a black hole and I had made that. I felt like walking down the street again and standing in that darkness feeling safe. The clock on the church tower showed half past ten, the last bus from Ålborg came rattling up from Søndergade and passed us before it turned down to the coach station on the other side of the church. We watched the red rear lights disappear, it had filled the evening with sound and then it was quiet and I clearly heard the sea behind all the houses and I thought: how silent this town is, and yet never silent. But Jesper turned round and said:

"Oh, no, not again." And then I heard it too, hooves on the cobblestones and squeaking wheels. It was Baron Biegler's black landau. The two horses looked worn out with foam on their flanks, and when the carriage drove past you could see the coat of arms had fallen off the door and it was so close we could smell the reek of frightened horses. The carriage stopped just ten metres in front of us outside the Music House, the door was flung open and Baron Biegler got out in his sheepskins that were not so white any more, and he had something big and heavy in his arms.

"It's a gramophone," whispered Jesper and the baron lifted it up high so I could easily feel its weight right up to where I was standing and he threw it in through the window.

"It doesn't even work!" he yelled while the splinters of glass hung for a moment before crashing into the shop, and if a grown man could weep, that was what I heard. He was blind drunk. On his way back into the carriage he stumbled on the step and fell forwards, and the groan I heard made me think of huge animals, elephants or rhinoceros with wrinkled lifeless skin falling down into the hunter's pit.

"He doesn't need any help, that one," said Jesper, "he's beaten by his own machine. Bankrupt, kaput, finished. I'm sure he couldn't pay for that gramophone. All his money has gone into booze. Idiot!" And then the carriage vanished as swiftly as it had come, not towards the Aftenstjernen, not back to Bangsbo, but up towards the railway station.

"Where d'you think he's going?"

"To the scrapheap of history," said Jesper.

It was all over in an instant. On the church tower the clock still showed half past ten, and it struck once as we walked past. At the same moment we heard fog horns hooting from the harbour and fog came drifting up Tordenskjoldsgade, Lodsgade, Havngade, it fell silently over Fiskerklyngen in Gamle Fladstrand where the hero Terje Vigen landed in Ibsen's long poem. Soon only the street lamps rose clear and shone down on a mass that devoured everything, people and houses, we could not see more than three metres in front of us. The lights around us were hard to make out and Jesper stayed where he was; stretching out his arms like a blind man he said:

"This is what it must have been like when the Man from Danzig was shipwrecked. He must have been frightened. He thought he knew where everything was, and then it was all sheer chaos. Put your hand in front of your eyes, Sistermine, and spin round three times, then tell me which is the way home."

I did as he said, I spun around so I almost fell down, I opened my eyes and peered in all directions.

"I don't know."

"Then anything can happen."

He still stood with his arms out feeling around for our route as if in doubt before finally deciding and saying:

"Come on, we'll try this way," but I do not think he was ever in doubt. We turned right and I thought I could glimpse the shape of Tordenskjold's House in Skippergade, and that street led back the way we had come, just further east and nearer the sea. We walked carefully, reverently, I thought, as if at a funeral, and then the fog horn struck our bodies, for there was nothing to cut it off, there was nothing but cold vapour everywhere, my stomach felt shivery and the damp air covered my face and made me shudder even though my coat was warm and covered my knees.

"It's cold," I said.

"It's colder in Spain."

"What are you talking about? Oranges grow in Spain."

94

"Not in the mountains. The earth is frozen so hard there you can't dig trenches, so the Fascist hunters have easy targets. The eleventh battalion have so few weapons left now the new volunteers have to wait till a comrade falls before they get a gun."

I tried to fill the fog with uniformed men in a frozen Spain, but the fog was only fog.

"And d'you know what they write home about?"

"No."

"They run around in the snow with hardly any weapons freezing their bums off and then they write: "Send more chocolate!" Bloody hell! Maybe we should rob a shop. We could do Fru Sandbjerg's in Felledvej, she's a stupid cow anyway. Her shelves are bursting with chocolate." His arms cut through the fog, they were still stretched out, he turned, walked backwards, and I said:

"Would you like to have gone?"

"Yes."

He was too young, I knew, but if I tried hard I could see the top of the cranes at the shipyard sticking up out of the blanket of fog and I heard the echo of our shoes on the cobblestones, and now everything was of a greater age than us both and all that was ours had sunk into the earth, was dead and buried except for Jesper's voice. I closed my eyes and the night filled with Italian bombers and blown-up bridges, black smoke and grey stones against grey snow and roofless houses against a snow-grey sky and General Franco's forbidding bandolier and names like Jamara, Guadalajara, Brunete, and Teruel in ruins and always black horses dead in the snow and Jesper dead in the snow with his hands frozen fast in a victorious movement; "Viva la Muerte! This way, Sistermine, we'll soon be home."

But many never came back, and would anyone inherit Jesper's gun?

I felt ill, I said:

"Jesper, I feel ill, I'll have to sit down." And I sat down on the steps to a house, although I had no idea where it was. The walls were glistening with cold, but I unbuttoned my coat at the neck and took off my scarf. I'm going to be sick, I thought, and then I *was* sick, hard lumps of milk at the side of the steps. It hurt, my throat was blocked and I thought of Grandfather in the byre and Irma in the red dress and Lone in her red dress, both of them faceless in the same mirror in a dark room that was the whole world, and then I began to weep.

"Well, damn it, my dress is blue," I said aloud, suddenly angry, and I was sick again and felt better at once and still colder.

"I'm freezing."

"You're always freezing, what will you do in Siberia? Come with me to Morocco. We'll go as soon as the war's over."

"It's different in Siberia. It's not like here, they wear different clothes and have warm houses built of wood. Anyway, Franco crossed over from Morocco, I've read that."

"Not the Fascists' Morocco, the Arabs' Morocco, you fool. I'm going to Meknés, Marrakech, to the Morocco of the caravans and the Moors."

"Send me a postcard," I said. I wiped my mouth and started to laugh. He bent down and tied my scarf round my neck, put my beret on straight, pulled my coat collar up.

"Better now?"

"Yes," I said, and he took my hands and pulled me to my feet. "Which war?" I said.

"The Spanish one, and the one that will follow it if the Fascists win." But that was enough war for tonight, I put my arm through his and we walked through the fog that was familiar now, the town fell into place, the shipyard and fishmeal factory and the fish auction was on the left and the slaughterhouse straight ahead and Damsgaard the butchers on the right, I could smell myself forward.

"I know where we are," I said. "Why did we have to walk halfway round the town to get back here? We could have gone straight down Lodsgade."

"We had to avoid the Bible belt, that's Lillemor's mine-field, anything could have happened. Now we're safe."

Said the candidate for the International Brigades.

9

Havnegade runs parallel with Lodsgade a block further south, from the crossroads where Danmarksgade runs into Søndergade, to the square in front of the Cimbria Hotel by the harbour, and together the two streets and the houses between them form our town's counterpart to Nyhavn in Copenhagen. With the possible exception of Aftenstjernen this is where all the sins congregate. Færgekroen, the Ferry Inn, and Tordenskjolds Kro are in Lodsgade; at the Cimbria the bar at the rear is called Lodsgade 16 by finer folk and Rompa, The Arse, by everyone else, after that part of the body which is vital when you need to rid yourself of superfluous fluid. In Havnegade there is a new-style bodega and the Vinkælderen, the Wine Cellar, two houses up from the hotel and one staircase down. The only threat is my mother who has moved in here and observes life from the window on the first floor when she is not behind the counter of the dairy. Those who can bring themselves to raise their eyes when the night is far advanced can see her behind the curtain Bible in hand looking out, with her lips moving in prayer or exorcism.

"It's not much fun to be caught out like that," says Jesper, for sometimes she goes downstairs and out to the gateway, and more than one person who has had one over the eight has felt her wrath and sensed the flames of hell licking tentatively beneath his soles. It's hot, they think, and it's embarrassing, so when Jesper is going out at night he always makes a long detour and approaches his objective from another angle, even when he is only going one street away.

And that is what we're doing now. We negotiate Lodsgade on the lower side and walk along beside the Cimbria Hotel, there's laughter inside and people sitting at the windows, an icy wind sweeps in from the sea and blows away the fog and I can see the masts of the fishing boats tossing like inverted pendulums and hear them chafing against the sides of the wharf.

The first thing I see on the way down the steps to Vinkælderen is Uncle Nils. He is wearing a suit and a newly-ironed white shirt and he is not in clogs but narrow black shoes I haven't noticed before. It's too late to turn round, people behind me are pushing and Jesper keeps a tight hold of my arm. Uncle Nils hangs up his coat on a hook in the cloakroom, he straightens his tie and glances up the steps. He smiles.

"Why, here we have Jesper," he says, lifting his hand in salute.

"Hi, Uncle Nils," says Jesper. I do not say anything. I am waiting, stiff with fright. I'm only just fourteen and on the way down to the Vinkælderen at half past eleven at night and my uncle stands on the steps.

"Good evening, young lady." He bows deeply and I giggle without meaning to and bob carefully. I look at Jesper, but he's busy taking off his new coat, and then he helps me with mine like a perfect gentleman, looking delighted the whole time.

Uncle Nils is different tonight. He smiles and chats, but out on the farm and in the fields and on the driver's seat behind the horse he's always moody with a deep furrow between his eyes, and he hardly ever utters a word. Now the furrow has vanished and he is looking great, less than a year older than my father, for he was Grand-mother Hedvig's youngest son, and she died when he was born. I can see from him that my father isn't that old. He's already had a schnaps, or two or three, he is red in the face and he bows again and throws out his arm.

"Shall we go in?"

"What's it like in there?"

"There's a good few down there."

"And you've had a few, too, most likely," says Jesper, and I am afraid Uncle Nils will be cross at that, but he is not.

"That was a good one," he says. "I'm celebrating, you see, I've made an important decision, so it called for one or two under the hat." He puts his hand to his head, he's hatless, his short fair hair is curly and he has put something on it which makes it shine in the lamplight. He chuckles and throws out his hand again.

"After you, ladies and gents. Don't let's waste precious time."

Jesper runs his fingers through his curly hair to make it tidier, I can't see it makes any difference. He pulls at his sleeves and takes my arm again and we go down yet another flight of steps and into the room. It's long and narrow and hot after the raw air of Havnegade. There are shallow windows just under the ceiling, and at the far end there's a dance floor with a dais in front with deserted instruments on it, the band is having a rest or has not yet started. Four men in identical jackets are at the bar, each with a beer in his hand. The place is more than half full, but along the wall at the far end there are some empty tables. It's a long way to go and we have to walk past a lot of people. Uncle Nils points and wants to go in. I stop, I can't do it, I do not feel well.

"I must go to the toilet."

"Go on then," says Jesper, "I'll stay here just outside and wait for you. Take all the time you need."

The toilet is near the entrance, to the right of where we stand. There is a wash basin in there and a mirror and two cubicles. I go into one and sit down on the lavatory lid. I sit there a few minutes thinking, maybe I'll be sick again, perhaps that's what it is. I try, and a little bit comes, but mostly because I am forcing myself. Then I pull the chain and go out to the basin and splash my face with water. I look at myself in the mirror. I have a high forehead and a snood above my temples. It is practical with hair like mine but it makes me look well-scrubbed and shiny and childish sometimes. Like now. I lean forwards. A pale girl of fourteen, not a second older. I look down at my dress to see if there are any spots of sick on it, but there are none, and then someone comes in. I see her in the glass, a lady in a green dress, her blonde hair shines and she smiles with red lips.

"Hallo," she says. I do not reply, I don't know her. She

stands there behind me. I think, she's going to touch me, and then she puts her hands on my shoulders and says:

"Let's have a look at you." I turn round passively. The only light is above the mirror, and I throw a shadow over her face as she bends forward and looks closely at mine. She is an adult and very attractive and I can't manage to feel anything but fourteen.

"May I?" she says and doesn't wait for an answer. I do not give one. She takes off the snood and puts it in her mouth, uses her fingers as a comb and pulls my hair forwards, it's a good feeling, no one has done anything like it since I was little, my head just follows and I look down at the floor. It's best like that. Then she puts the snood back, straight above my ear so my fringe hangs loose at the side, one ear is hidden by hair, the other uncovered. I often have my ears showing with a rubber band round my pony tail at the back, but it has never felt like it does now.

"Up with your mouth and tighten your lips," she says. She's slightly taller than I am, she has green eyes and high cheek bones and small ears close to her head. I put my head back a little, afraid she will think I'm surrendering to her, open my mouth a little and tighten my lips against my teeth. I do not know why I let her go on, I've never seen her before, an unknown face is close to mine and I close my eyes as if she's going to kiss me and I would *like* her to. Some women are like that, I am not, but when something touches my lips I start to tremble. I open my eyes and she smiles and says:

"Stand quite still now," while she carefully draws the

red lipstick across my mouth, – "there." I close my eyes again and do not tremble any longer. She is welcome to go on.

"Rub your lips against each other, then you can look in the mirror." I do as she says; with a strange soft feeling, wanting to keep my mouth slightly open. I turn round and look in the mirror. I look grown up and a little wistful, like someone with a secret, hidden years that cannot be talked about, fantastic events maybe, someone who has travelled far and seen things no one but she understands. I smile at the reflection and draw a breath. I think, my mother has never used lipstick.

She is behind me in the mirror, she lifts my hair, lets her fingers slide through it and our eyes meet in the glass. Someone ought to clean that mirror, I think, but even so she sees who I am, and it does not matter.

"Jesper was quite right," she says, "it didn't take much."

"Do you know Jesper?"

"I certainly do." She lets her eyes slide over me and smiles with the red mouth that is like mine now.

"You've got a good body, you're fine here," she says and takes hold of both her breasts with hands that have red nails, laughs aloud and pushes them up in a way I would never have done, and then I blush.

"That's right, now you've got a bit of colour in your cheeks. That's how it should be."

"I had to!" says Jesper, "we wouldn't have been served otherwise. You looked like a scared twelve-year-old. You don't look like that now," he grins. "You look just smashing." I blush again and straighten my back, and we walk together in among the tables, people turn in their chairs and watch us on our way to the long wall where Uncle Nils sits. He waves to us.

"At least she didn't have net stockings."

"Net stockings? Jytte? What are you on about? Why the hell should Jytte wear net stockings?"

Uncle Nils is moving into town. He has found work at the shipyard and a little attic flat in Søndergade. He pours beer from the bottle into his glass, raises the glass and says:

"Here's to a new life. Raise your glasses!" Jesper and I do that and we drink together. I'm so thirsty I could drink anything. All the moisture has left my body, it vanished with the fog out in the streets and the beer is bitter and cold and refreshing.

"Ah, it'll be good to get away from that old witch, if you'll pardon the expression. I'm never going out to Vrangbæk again, not even for Christmas. I'm never going to pick up a pitchfork again, never sit behind a horse as long as I live. I'm going to buy a scooter as soon as I've got enough money, and until then I'll walk. Everywhere! A free proletarian who won't take shit from anyone! Ho, ho.' He downs the rest of his beer in one gulp and Jesper follows suit and they slam down their glasses on the table and say in chorus:

"Well, that didn't hurt, did it?" And my beer doesn't hurt either, even though I drink slower and don't slam down my glass. I catch myself sitting smiling at the woman called Jytte a few tables away, she winks at me and I smile more broadly and it does not matter that Uncle Nils calls my grandmother a witch. If I had known it was all right I should have said it long ago. It doesn't seem to worry Jesper either, he says:

"But here we sit with three empty glasses, that wasn't what we ordered, was it?"

"No, no, that's all wrong, we'll soon change that," says Uncle Nils and picks up the bottles in one hand and waves them in the air so the glass clinks to tell the waitress to bring more. Soon three full bottles are on the table. Uncle Nils is in fine fettle and pours out for us before we can do it ourselves, and then we have to skål again.

"Welcome to the town then, Uncle Nils," I say, I feel I ought to. "First it was our father, and now it's you. Maybe everyone will come soon," but instead of raising his glass Uncle Nils stops smiling. He leans forward so one of the bottles falls over, he is drunk, beer runs over the table, but he does not care, he just grips my arm and squeezes it so I am almost frightened.

"But don't you two understand anything? Magnus *wanted* to stay at Vrangbæk. He wanted to be a farmer and nothing else. He slaved like a dog to please those two, I've never seen anyone work so hard, it was painful," he says, his eyes fill and the musicians are on the dais starting to play so he has to lean further forward while two couples make their way on to the dance floor, and he raises his voice:

"But that damned witch wouldn't look at him, would never touch him or talk to him, and as soon as he could manage on his own he was sent off to town. And the old man let it happen, blessed be his memory, that randy old goat, if you'll pardon the expression." Uncle Nils stops talking, he looks down at his hand clutching my arm, the skin is white on both sides right down to the fingers, and he lets go and says:

"I beg your pardon, I'm sorry, I hurt you, I didn't mean to."

"It's nothing," I say, rubbing my arm cautiously, the blood runs again and it smarts and stings right up to above the elbow.

"Yes, it is. I've had too much to drink tonight, I must go home now." He rises heavily, another bottle falls over and Jesper catches it in flight and gets to his feet too.

"Don't go, Uncle Nils, stay here with us for a while."

"No, this ought to be a joyful day for me and I don't want to spoil it. It was a pleasure to meet you here and not at Vrangbæk, and I understand it's a secret." He smiles faintly.

"Besides, I haven't too far to go home now."

"Welcome all the same, though."

"Thank you. And forget those things I said."

He walks between the tables looking rather like the old Uncle Nils, but not entirely. I turn to Jesper who is still standing up.

"What was all that about?"

"Nothing. Nothing I haven't thought about before. I'm not stupid after all." Then he bows gallantly and says:

"Come on, let's dance."

We drink what's left in our glasses and go out on the

dance floor. There are a lot of people there now and the music is loud and there is laughter at the tables and at one of them everyone is singing in chorus. I am not stupid either, no one can say that, and I think of my father out in the fields with his back slowly growing bent and Grandfather in the barn swinging to and fro and Grandmother's rigid face in the shadows, she is there watching him throw the rope over the beam and standing up on the stool, but she does not stop him, I can't understand why and I do not know if that is exactly true. Maybe it's something I have dreamt, but that is what I see and there's something wrong about it. It doesn't matter, though, for what I chiefly feel is two bottles of beer on an empty stomach and at some tables the ladies are looking at Jesper, I realise they do not know who I am, for they look at me too, and it's obvious they hate me with all their hearts. That makes me laugh out loud. Jesper whirls me around to the music, I feel his firm hand on my back. Everyone knows who *he* is, and I am the secret woman.

II

10

I was fourteen and a half when the Germans came. On that 9th April we woke to the roar of aeroplanes swooping so low over the roofs of the town that we could see the black iron crosses painted on the underside of their wings when we leaned out of the windows and looked up. The Danish warship *Peder Skram* was anchored in the roads outside the harbour, but it merely lay there silently and did not fire a single shot.

It was still cold then, it had been a hard winter that year with ice-breakers along the coast and inside the breakwater, gusts of wind blew in from the west across the mainland from the North Sea, and there was still snow in drifts on the fields and on the roads out to the farms and in Vannverk forest up to the Flade Bakker and the church where my grandfather lay in the graveyard.

In the afternoon a man came cycling down Lodsgade. He wore a cap with ear warmers and a scarf round his neck.

"They're coming! They're coming!" he shouted. I thought I had heard that shout before. We got up from the table leaving the layer cake where it was and went up the road together. We were not the only ones. Fishermen and shipyard workers came from the harbour in overalls, the door of Færgekroen flew open and the staff came out with the proprietor leading, he was already drunk, and Herlov Bendiksen came to his door with the apron over his stomach sparkling with tiny splinters of glass when he stood still and even more when he started to walk. Soon there was a small procession of silent people, I heard nothing but their steps on the cobblestones, and we crowded together on the pavement to see the first column arrive. Nothing came, so we went on along Danmarksgade almost up to Nytorv and came to a stop just opposite the offices of the local paper. A figure came rushing out of the door, he tore down the latest posters fastened to a notice board on the wall and left everything blank and bare where there had always been something before. It was my brother Jesper. He called:

"Hi, Sistermine!' right across the street and waved, and I waved back. He looked around and then bent down with his hands on his knees and his rump towards the direction from where those approaching would soon enter the town from the south. A man started to laugh and soon everyone standing there was laughing. It was a strange and lonely sound among the buildings, otherwise all was quiet, and Jesper raised a clenched fist in greeting.

"No pasaran, they shall not pass!" he shouted, and vanished inside again as quickly as he had come out.

Only my father did not laugh. He took me by the shoulder and said:

"You must show you are Danish children now." He was confused, after all it was only me standing there and he had forgotten I was no longer a child. I had been having periods for almost three years and had stopped growing a year ago too, but I had forgotten about it myself, and he probably just meant we should behave normally as they had told us to on the wireless.

"Yes, of course we shall," I said, "we'll just stand here quite quietly looking at them, and we shan't even smile."

We stood there a long time. No one came. In the end a few people went home, and then my father did, but I stayed there gazing at the door across the street.

Three men came out. The first two walked calmly along the pavement, the third looked to right and left before he started to run round the house and into an alleyway with a brown paper parcel under his arm. And then Jesper came. He saw me at once and came straight across. His face looked drawn and he walked quickly, and I heard the slap of his heels on the road that was quiet again.

"Come on," he said, taking my arm, "we'll go on home." The few people still standing about looked anxiously at his face, but he would not say anything before we were further down the street. It was like a film at the Palace Theatre; groups of people whispering to each other, the queue in front of the savings bank where everyone wanted to draw their money out, frightened eyes behind window panes. Jesper glanced over his shoulder before he leaned towards me and said:

"The Germans have killed five Danish soldiers at the border."

I saw five bodies lying at the spot where Helga and I had planned to embrace each other, the line was invisible now, the bodies covered it completely and streams of blood ran out on each side as if from a hilltop and down into each country, and one of those who did the shooting might have been Walter.

"So we're at war then?"

"At war? I don't think anyone is going to war in this bloody country! Haven't you heard Stauning on the radio? Behave naturally! Those five were sacrificed for appearance's sake. It was murder. And now we must behave naturally."

"Where did you hear all this?"

"I do work on a newspaper. We have got a telephone, damn it."

When we went through the gateway in Lodsgade we did not go upstairs to the flat but on across the yard to the rack where our cycles were, and we pulled them out and rode into the street again and took a zigzag route on side streets until we came to the end of the town to the south. At each block we looked down into the main street to check, but there was no German column there yet. At Møllehuset we had to go out on to the main road to Sæby, for everywhere else was impassibly slippery because of ice and in some places the snow had been blown into drifts across the roads. It was a cold spring and I was frozen to the marrow and defenceless on my cycle when we came out into the open at Bangsbostrand, quite alone on the road with the cold grey sea right in and nothing between us and what was coming. Jesper rode very fast and I kept up, I had made good use of the hours on the goods cycle, but if he was impressed he did not show it.

Just this side of Understed, midway between our town and Sæby, Jesper braked, got off his bike and squatted down to listen. I did the same. What we heard was the future. A faint drone through the cold, a drone that rose without a sign of fading again, an irreversible drone and Jesper straightened up with a shaking body and rubbed his shoulders before he looked out at the coast. A steep slope led down to the shore from the road with rough sheets of ice all along the edge, and he turned and looked up at the gentle slopes of Understed. The low houses with their red roofs could just be seen over the rise, and the little school called Vangen was hidden in a clump of trees. My father had been a pupil there for several years, in shorts and a peaked cap, to and fro from Vrangbæk which was further inland. I had cycled that way many times. It was a long way, but his back was still straight then.

A cart track partly covered with snow wound up over the fields, and Jesper pointed and said:

"That's the only possibility. We'll nip up there. Fast."

It was hard to pedal, so we dismounted and pushed the bikes all the way up to a grass field where the cart track came to an end, I felt my breath tearing at my throat and heard Jesper panting in front of me. At the top there was a heap of manure which had just begun to thaw out and would be spread on the fields as soon as spring really came. If it came. From the field we had a good view of the road in both directions and the grey shadow of the *Peder Skram* out in the roads lying completely still, and we saw the thin floury layer of ice on the beach, a peaceful veil between land and water. And then the Germans came.

First two motorcycles with machine guns sticking up from the side cars and only the helmets of the soldiers holding the weapons visible, and then came armoured vehicles and lorries with soldiers in the back in two rows facing each other and cannons on trailers and two cars with heavy machine guns on the roof and then more lorries, everything in an endless row of helmets without faces and an endless roar that swallowed up all space around it so I could not tell if I was breathing. And perhaps I was not breathing, for there was not enough air left for anyone else. But I heard Jesper sobbing, thin and sharp, he was white in the face and clutching his throat as if he was being strangled. And then the tears came gushing in two straight streams from his eyes. He wiped his nose and sobbed again and again, completely out of control like a little brother. I looked down at the shining column that rolled along, forbidding and unswerving on its way to our town, and I realised that *No pasaran!* was meaningless now, that was what Jesper saw, that it was too late. Then I started to weep too. I leaned against the seat of my bicycle, for my legs would not hold me up any longer, the roar made them tremble and quiver, made the whole earth shake.

At my side Jesper let go of his bicycle and began to talk, quietly at first and then louder and louder.

"Bloodiest hell," he said, "the devil in blackest hell, flaming devilish hell," and when I looked up he had dug his hands into the half-melted outer layer of the muck heap. He tore big pieces out and threw them down the slope, and even though they didn't reach far I was afraid the soldiers would turn round and see us and mow us down where we stood without any protection, because he yelled as well:

"The future is shit," he yelled, the tears pouring down, "the future is bloody shit, just like this. Take this, you Nazi swine! Do you hear!" And he pulled more half-frozen lumps from the heap and hurled them as far as he could, but they did not hear him. Not one helmet moved and the gun barrels pointed straight up at the sky. Then Jesper gave up. He stood there with his hands at his sides and lumps of cow muck right up his arms. He was gasping for breath and blinking and blinking and I took the few steps over to him and dried his cheeks with my handkerchief.

"I wish," I said aloud, "I wish one of those vehicles would drive right off the road and disappear." And I had barely finished before we heard a roaring from down there. One of the lorries had driven too far out, its back wheels spun on the ice sheets and the back where the soldiers sat slid over the edge and the roar we heard was the wheels in thin air. And then the lorry vanished, rear first down the slope to the shore, and the soldiers yelled and jumped out on each side.

No one seemed to have been hurt, but one link in the unbreakable chain was suddenly missing.

"Well I'll be damned, Sistermine," said Jesper between two deep breaths – "that wasn't bad," and he smiled for the first time that day.

11

Two German soldiers stand on the quay weeping. They don't stand together, but on each side of the gangway of a troopship. One of them faces Pikkerbakken behind the town, the other the shipyard, but I do not know if they see anything at all. They are young, not much older than Jesper, and they are being sent to Norway. There is a war on in Norway, in Denmark it is quiet. They have had a good time in Denmark.

"They drink the cream straight out of the bucket," my father says and means it literally.

"They just come straight in from the street and drink the cream out of the bucket." He has a grey moustache now and his temples are grizzled, I think he looks stylish and he blows cigar smoke into the air and the wind throws it back into my eyes until the tears start to run. I see the world through the same haze as the soldiers, the grey-green uniforms are wavering, it's irritating, I blink hard, and the one who is looking at the shipyard moves his lips.

"What's that he's saying?"

"He's saying mutti, "mamma."

"I'd never say that. I would never stand here crying and saying mamma," I say, wiping my eyes with the sleeve of my jacket.

"Maybe, maybe not," says my father. He has just told me I shan't be able to go on to gymnasium. That's why we're out for a walk. I am the best pupil leaving from Middle School. I had Excellent for my main mark.

"We have discussed it and we agree," he says and means my mother and himself, but of course I know she is the one who decided. He is just loyal.

"I can work in the evenings, and in the holidays. I can manage, I'm strong."

"I'm sure you can. But it's not just the money. There's the war as well."

"What war? Hardly anyone fights in this country." I turn towards one of the soldiers and shout:

"NO ONE DARES TO FIGHT IN THIS COUNTRY!"

"Hush, girl! What are you thinking of?" He doesn't know what to do so he puts his hand over my mouth. His hand smells of wood shavings and polish. I take his hand away and he doesn't stop me.

"But it's true! And he doesn't understand what I say. They've been here two years and don't understand a word of Danish. All they do is march, dig trenches and bathe at Frydenstrand." My stomach knots up and I take a step towards the one who said mamma.

"Kommst du von Magdeburg? Heisst du Walter? Ist Helga die Name deiner Schwester?" He turns slowly, his eyes are full of tears, his nose is red and he dries his eyes with the back of his hand like a child.

"Nein," he says, shaking his head.

"Idiot," I say, and he understands *that*. I can *see* him drying up. He seizes the strap of his gun and his expression changes. My father grips my shoulder and mutters fiercely in my ear:

"Now we're just going to walk calmly, do you hear?" His big hand clenches my collar bone, it hurts and the whole time we're walking I feel the soldier behind us, his hand on his gun, my father's stiff gait and hard body. I have the sun in my face, it is blinding and my eyes are swimming, but I do not raise my arm, I blink and blink but it doesn't help. It is June but I feel the raw air at my back as if the ice lay thick up to the breakwater in wicked floes, the whole harbour frozen over again, no way out.

When we get to the harbour square in front of the hotel, I tear myself free and let him go up Lodsgade alone to where my mother is bound to be standing at the window waiting. The shop is shut for the day and a stream of blue-clad workers comes cycling from the shipyard. He said we should just go for a walk, and I agreed, for it was a long time since I last heard his voice without anyone else's filling the cramped apartment.

I stop in Skippergade and look back. My father is still standing in the square with his hands at his sides and the dead cigar in his mouth. He does not know which way to go. He looks like a poor man, a childless man without shelter, quite alone in the world, and I think I must go down to him again, say it does not matter, that nothing matters. But that is not true.

The German ship lies hidden behind the shipyard cranes and I see there is no ice in the harbour basin nor on the sea, but from where I stand the opening in the breakwater is out of sight. Only two long arms stick up from north and from south and join in a ring around our town and hold it fast.

My father stands on the square for a long time. I stand still as long as he does, looking at him. He knows I am there, but he does not turn my way. We wait for each other. In the end he lights his cigar again and starts to walk slowly along past the Cimbria and up into Havnegade instead of going home. Maybe to the Vinkælderen or to a place in Søndergade where he plays billiards now. He has not been to Aftenstjernen since we moved from the north of the town. Then I also turn round and hurry up Lodsgade. I see my mother out of the corner of my eye, she stands at the window looking down into the street waiting as I expected, but I do not look up. Just go into the yard for my bicycle and bowl off before she can get down to the gateway.

I take Rosevej out of town to the Seamen's School. Lone's father stands outside the fence clipping the hedge. I look straight ahead and try to get past without him noticing, but he turns and calls out:

"Good evening, young lady, see you in the autumn!" He used to be head teacher at the primary school, now he is principal of the gymnasium and like everyone else he thinks I am going on there. My results were in the local paper, they always publish the marks of the best pupil, and it was Jesper who typeset the notice. He had put an eye-catching frame round my name, with the marks, so they could be seen the moment you opened up at page two. It was embarrassing, I did not go out for three days.

My best work up to now, said Jesper, he had wanted to use Gothic type to make the announcement even more impressive, but there were not enough characters left. The Germans had worn them out, and when I thought of it afterwards I felt it made it look too much like a death notice.

Lone's father is just Hans's father now, and I do not understand why he talks to me, I have been taboo for several years. But perhaps he has not many friends left. He is a member of Denmark's National Socialist Workers Party, and some workers' party that is, says Jesper,

"Where the best-known toilers are Count Bent Holstein, Count Knut Knuthenborg, Count Rathlau and Sehested, Master of the Royal Hunt. And they are not even Danish, but imported from the south, like foot and mouth disease." Many farms have had a taste of that. Every single cow at Vrangbæk had to be slaughtered and Grandmother has sold the farm and moved into a home for old sourpusses at Sæby, where she sits in a chair all day long heaping insults on anyone who dares go near her.

So Vrangbæk has gone for good, and no one grieves over that except my mother who can be heard to utter her eternal:

"He might have given us a house, you know."

All that is behind us now, we do not cycle that way any more, but at night I ride Lucifer along the paths in the Chinese garden behind the house. It has grown into a forest of sky-high trees and there is a sun and a moon at the same time there. Lucifer's hooves clatter over the wooden bridges and I am hot and sweaty and feel the wind on my chest and the horse rocking between my legs, and I grip hard with my thighs and lean forward holding tight to his mane so as not to fall off.

But the Chinese garden has been demolished and turned into a gravel pit to sell sand and gravel at high prices to the Germans, who need quantities when they build bunkers and tank traps and defences for the South Battery in the hills near Understed. But none of this makes any difference to Lone's father, for he has chosen another country than ours, and I bowl past and call out:

"Wir sehen uns niemals, Herr Oberhauptbahnhof," thinking that is one for him. But it doesn't give me any pleasure, indeed I should have been glad to see him at the gymnasium in Hjørring in the autumn, and when I turn round I see a melancholy Nazi in the road, shears in hand, who fraternises with the Germans because they take a scientific view of life and see the potential of ants in the human world.

My friend Marianne lives in a brick-built house where the town ends and the farm lands begin, past the nobs and the white fences, past the Seamen's School and out on the windswept heath behind Nordre Strandvej. Jesper's old shack is not much further as the crow flies, but to get there you have to cycle along the Elling brook inland to the bridge on Skagensvejen and then right along the field path again on the other side. That's the good thing about that shack. Few people bother to go there.

If Lone came from a home with a grand piano and I from one with a cinema piano, Marianne is from a home with a jew's harp. She has five unruly brothers younger than herself, her mother is dead and her father is a carter. That's what he calls himself; Carter Larsen. All through the winter he combs the beaches for driftwood, he clears away trees blown down by gales in autumn storms, and sometimes in the dark he goes into Vannverks forest getting wood illegally. Then he cuts it up into suitable lengths and splits it and puts it into big piles to dry all around the yard, the scent makes me go numb. When autumn comes he drives around selling it in sacks and cord measures to people who will buy in a town where coke is the usual fuel for the stove, but now dried peat because trade with England has stopped. There is not much money in that.

At first he had a horse and cart, then a small lorry he kept in the stable, and now he has a horse again because petrol is rationed. The lorry and the horse share the stable. The lorry rusts on the side where the salt-laden wind blows in from the sea, and the horse kicks at the other when he feels cramped. That is what I remember best from that place; the scent of wood drying in the sun and the horse whinnying in the stable and the crack of its iron shoes striking the lorry. He is called Jeppe after Jeppe of the Hill in Holberg's play because he is so thirsty and neither the lorry nor Jeppe will be moved because Carter Larsen knows his horse and believes he has a right to kick.

"He's good to animals, I'll say that for him," says Marianne, and leaves it at that.

When she was thirteen her mother died and Marianne

took her place and proved she could do it, she had no choice, otherwise the social would have come to take her brothers and place them like silver foxes on farms in the district. People call it that because it provides extra income for farmers, like keeping foxes does.

Marianne has cigarettes and beer. I borrow a swimsuit from her and we cycle to the bathing place north of Frydenstrand. The German soldiers have built a wooden bathing jetty that reaches out beyond the third sandbank where the water is deep. We sit on the beach in the shelter of a dune and smoke Virginia cigarettes Marianne has got hold of, I don't know where they came from, and we each drink a Tuborg and watch the soldiers swim and dive. They look at us as they run past, and it's hard not to show off a bit. They're like small boys at holiday camp. They don't look so dangerous without their uniforms. I smile, but I hate them.

I stub out the cigarette in the loose sand and take a big gulp of beer. It tastes flat and warm. "Have you ever seen such cocky young roosters?" says Marianne.

"A lot of them will be going to Norway soon. Then they won't be quite so full of themselves."

A tall fair soldier runs by, he smiles and waves, but I've done with smiling for today.

"It's a shame really. That one's got smashing thighs on him." Marianne waves back.

"Put a sock in it. They are the enemy, for God's sake."

"Do you think I don't know that? But he *is* good-looking. He's bound to have a young wife in Germany.

125

She sits at home listening to Sara Leander on the radio and knitting warm socks with a blond baby inside her. And now he's going up to those ferocious Norwegians, and maybe the socks won't get there in time. Poor thing."

She's trying to get out of an awkward situation, I can hear that, but all the same I get mad. But Marianne is my best friend now, so I just say:

"When the war's over I'm going travelling."

"You may still be at gymnasium. You know you're the hope of us all, our only one." Marianne is to start work as a shop assistant at Damsgaard's in the autumn. It cost a lot of free wood, but now it's all fixed. I am, or *was*, the only one outside the white fences with a "future".

"I'm not going to gymnasium. I'm not allowed to."

"What?"

"I'm not allowed to go. I don't care, I'll go off travelling anyway."

"Where are you going?"

"To Siberia."

"To Siberia? How are you going to get there? It's not possible."

"I'll join the communists and go to the Soviet Union, and then I'll get leave to go on the Trans-Siberian Railway."

"But you know there are prison camps in Siberia, don't you?"

"Nazi propaganda," I say, but it does not sound convincing and I am not certain. I'm not certain of anything.

"Don't be cross," I say, "I didn't mean you are a Nazi.

Got another cigarette?" Marianne has and she is not cross. I take one and light it, though I don't really feel like smoking any more, my mouth is dry and I think, I shouldn't have said that about Siberia. I don't know why I did, I haven't thought of Siberia for a long time. Now I must think of something to make her forget it and remember something else instead.

"You should have seen Jesper when he came home the other night," I say.

All the girls I know fancy Jesper, some make no secret of being in love with him. They have no shame, they lie in bed at night and think of him, they tell me and laugh. He's public property. I don't know when that came about.

Marianne raises her head. "Why is that?" she says.

I tell her, but I do not tell her everything.

When curfew began at ten o'clock that night Jesper was not in. He had been home after work, had his evening meal and gone out again. But we weren't worried, we thought he had gone to a friend's house and would go to work from there. He often does that, and I went to bed at eleven. I fell asleep, and in my dream someone knocked at the windowpane. It was a familiar sound. I got up and went over to the window of the attic at Vrangbæk and looked out into the Chinese garden. I knew Jesper was out there, that he was hanging from the roof, and I was afraid he would fall down, because he had hung there for a long time, several years. I opened the window and it was daylight. In the sunshine I saw the bulldozers demolishing the garden, and in front of one of the shovels Jesper was rolling round wearing an army coat. His face was badly wounded.

"JESPER!" I called, but he smiled and waved with bandaged hands.

"No pasaran, Sistermine," he said and his voice was so clear and calm that it calmed me too, and I thought everything was all right, he knew what he was doing, it was part of a plan I did not know about, so I closed the window, I was tired and wanted to go back to sleep. And then it was night again. I lay down under my quilt, but the knocking went on. I opened my eyes and got up. It was darker now, and it took a few moments for me to realise that this was because of the blackout curtains. I opened them and Jesper's face was close to the pane, one eye was black and swollen and blood ran from a cut on his cheek. He smiled as he had in the dream and whispered insistently:

"Open up for Christ's sake!"

I pulled at the catches and pushed the window up, gripped his jacket and pulled and dragged. He was heavy and did not help much, he was holding his hands to his chest and trying not to fall, and he just slid over the sill. Something fell out from under his jacket and hit the floor with a thud and Jesper fell after it with his hands held to his chest. It must have hurt him. I bent down quickly and picked up the thing he had dropped. It was a pistol, a Luger, and it was German. It was warm in my hands from his body and different from anything I had ever held, hard and real. Jesper crawled away and sat against the wall between the beds. He stretched out his hand and I gave him the pistol, and I must have looked frightened, for he pressed it to his chest and held it carefully as you hold a child and said:

"Calm down, he doesn't know he hasn't got it, anyway there were a lot of us, I'll never see him again." He wiped his cheek and got blood on his hand and he looked down at the blood as if it was something quite unexpected, and he picked up the pistol again and looked at it with the same surprise. Then he leaned his head against the wall and closed his good eye with the pistol on his lap.

"Yes, well," he said, "that's it. It's going to begin soon."

I do not tell Marianne about the pistol, nor about my dream, only that Jesper had been fighting a German soldier and what he looked like when I opened the window and he fell into the room and thumped the floor face down. And that's plenty. That is all Marianne will think about now.

"Poor Jesper. You bandaged his wounds, I expect?"

"Of course I did," I say, and that's true, but when I see Marianne's face I regret having said anything at all.

The wind has got up and it blows chill. It has changed from light airs to a stiff breeze and still more, coming from the north, and I feel gooseflesh break out on my thighs and back. I put the towel round my shoulders, crouch down and smoke the last of the cigarette, and the marram grass bends in the wind and fine grains of sand fly in my face and hair so I have to turn on my heels and talk backwards to Marianne.

"Shall we swim or just sit here?"

All the soldiers have come in from the jetty and gone up to the beach house to change. We can hear their voices and laughter behind the peeling walls. The strange tongue that I know but don't feel at home in makes me restless. I get to my feet and walk around. Marianne looks up at the sky. It is still just as blue.

"I'm not promising anything," she says.

It's still colder on the jetty. We clasp our arms around our bodies and walk slowly over the splintery boards, and Marianne says "Ow" every other step. She's two metres in front of me, she's reluctant and fussy. It irritates me. This day has been meaningless, unreal.

"We'll rub it out," Jesper would have said, "we'll just tear it out of the calendar"

"It can't be rubbed out," I say aloud.

"What can't be rubbed out?"

"Today can't be rubbed out."

"Why should it be?" Marianne turns round. I stop, I'm so cold my teeth are chattering. She puts her head on one side and looks me in the face.

"Oh, you really are in a bad way. To think I didn't see that at once!" She takes two steps backwards and puts her arms around me and drops her towel, and that helps a bit, just now. She is dry and warm and a shelter from the wind. I shut my eyes. When I open them again I see the fair-haired soldier over her shoulder. He must have been in the water as we went out or hiding under the jetty, and now he has climbed up at the far end and is looking back. Perhaps he is waiting for us. There are just the three of us out here now.

"Marianne," I say, "turn round."

She turns. "Oh ho," she says, "the man with the socks. There's no more cigarettes and beer. So it must be rape. Maybe our last hour has come."

"I don't think so."

He slides his heels on to the edge and balances on his toes and raises his arms straight out sideways. He is going to dive, he wants to show how clever he is, but he is not aware of the conditions. When we arrived it was high tide, now it is low. In half an hour the water drops by a metre, and it's not safe to dive there now. Not backwards anyhow. But he raises his arms to a point above his head, squats down and takes off and dives in a big arc backwards to vanish past the end of the jetty. We hold our breath and wait for him to come up again. But he does not come.

Marianne looks at me, biting her lips.

"It's too shallow there now, isn't it," she says.

We start to walk out. It's a long jetty, more than a hundred metres to the end, and we do not walk fast.

"Just think, he may be dead," says Marianne. I do not reply, I have to use what little will I have to go on. At last we stand on the very edge looking down into the water. He is floating there stretched out just under the surface, turning gently in the current from the Elling brook that runs out a little further north and along the shore here before turning out into the sea. It is completely silent, his fair hair waves back and forth.

"He's drowned," Marianne says in a small voice. Suddenly she cannot stand still. She clutches herself around the chest, she lets go and holds her chin as if she had toothache, she lifts one leg and puts it down again, she lifts the other and puts it down again.

"He's drowned, he's drowned," she whimpers.

"Not quite yet," I say.

He is unconscious, his mouth is open and from it small bubbles issue and rise to the surface. I think of smoke signals, messages from far away I have to interpret, and I force myself to be calm and concentrate and bend forward from my knees; I gaze at the bubbles, I listen.

"He is the enemy," Marianne says behind me.

That's true. I straighten up again. Perhaps the fact that the soldier is drowning now is part of the war. But no one is fighting in this country, not yet. The bubbles come more slowly, they stop, and then I jump.

I hit the water just by his arm and it reaches to my chest when I stand on the bottom. I am 1.62, he must be 1.90, and at first I step back, his white body looks horrible, and I think of the Man from Danzig on the sea bed, but then I get hold of his hair and lift his head to the surface, and hold him under the chin so his mouth is above water. He is not breathing now, but I start to pull him in. It is hard work and goes far too slowly because of all the resistance in the water, so I lie back and swim on my back, still holding him under the chin. I look up into the blue sky that spreads all over the world and it doesn't move, I'm not moving, and then I have to turn my head and count the posts along the jetty the whole way in so as not to lose my nerve. I can hear Marianne up on the planks, she's running to and fro calling, but I don't understand what. Maybe she's scolding. I don't care. I stop swimming when I feel the sandy bottom scraping my back. I put my head back until it rests and I want to stay like that, but his head is against my stomach. It's heavy and German, and I twist myself away and get hold of one of his arms and pull him up and out of the water. My legs shake, the wind is cold against my wet back and I think I'm not thinking. Marianne is behind me or maybe somebody else is, I can hear heavy breathing, but I do not turn round, I push the soldier over on to his side, put my finger in his mouth and straighten his tongue then push my knee down hard on his stomach several times until the water starts to run out and spread in a big dark patch over the white sand. I turn him over on his back, lower my head and put my lips over his lips and pinch his nose and blow air into his lungs at a steady rate. I keep on until my chest whistles, everything goes black and suddenly he coughs. I raise my head, I have saved his life. He was in the sea, and now he is as alive as Jesper by the breakwater when I pulled him up and out of the grasp of the Man from Danzig. But I have been closer to this enemy soldier than I have been to my brother, I can still feel it on my lips, and when I realise that I slap him hard on the face.

Marianne calls my name. I stand up slowly. All the soldiers have come out of the beach house, now they are standing motionless around me, they have their uniforms on, and they are looking down at my hand.

12

29th August 1943. At last!

Jesper went out in the morning, but not to work. Throughout the day there were riots and fights and explosions from sabotage actions in all the big towns. In Ålborg, German sharpshooters launched an attack to disperse the crowds. More than a hundred people were taken to hospital, thirteen of them dead.

He came home just before curfew. He looked exhausted, and I often thought afterwards that if he had been involved in so much it was no wonder he was tired. He had not organised all of it, of course, but he *had* been involved.

We had dinner in silence, except for the ticking of the clock on the wall and the clink of spoons. Once we heard a shot. My father stopped chewing and looked at the window, he clenched his jaws until they bulged on both sides, but Jesper did not lift his eyes from his plate. When he had finished eating he left the room.

When I went down to the bedroom soon afterwards he was already asleep.

All through the years a photograph of my mother and her family hung by the sofa in the living room above the dairy shop. Now *I* have it beside my own confirmation photograph and one of Jesper in uniform taken just after the war.

My maternal grandfather was a fisherman at Bangsbostrand. In the photograph he wears a suit and a white shirt with a high collar; his thin hair is combed back firmly and his big moustache has been brushed until it shines. He died before I was born. I have heard he was a right bastard. My grandmother is only forty-five but she looks older than I do today. Yet she is beautiful in a southern way, like an Italian belle, or, with the right dress, a Moroccan woman, like one of those Jesper saw at the foot of the mountains in front of their tent, with the flock of goats and the small children wrapped up in blue cloth so they will not be burned by the sun. The sun is the enemy there, like the cold in Siberia.

There were thirteen children plus Franz who died of Spanish influenza. In the picture the eldest is twenty-three, the youngest two. My mother is fourteen, and she is the only one with a natural smile. She has the round face of youth, and I can see we resemble each other, as fourteen-year-olds. Shortly after that she was saved, and she was faithful to the Bible until her death. My father could wound her but not rule over her. Never in my life did I see anything to match the twinkle in her eye in the family photograph.

She saw the world in images, and the images came from the Old Testament. Before 29th August 1943 the German soldiers were like the swarms of locusts in Egypt, a grey-green penance imposed on an unbelieving people, and when they came into the shop to buy milk, it was the eighth plague she saw. She bent her head and endured it, for it was sent by a stern and righteous God. But from that day forward they were the oppressors of all peoples, executioners of the Israelites, we all knew that, and her back grew straighter.

They were far more aggressive now, Denmark was under German administration, the populace was hostile, and when they came into the shop to buy or maybe *take* milk, she moved out from behind the counter, took her stand in the middle of the floor and pointed to the door saying:

"Heraus!" in a high hard voice that brooked no argument. She was half a metre shorter than most of them, but she was as thin and sharp as a knife and her gaze was so blue that they looked right through it and could not see themselves reflected, and then they grew dizzy and naked with uncertainty in their eyes. They backed towards the door staring at the tiles and mumbling insults in German we quite understood, but Lodsgade Dairy Shop was a closed oasis, they could not get past the little lady in the striped blue apron. I was sure they *saw* the flaming sword she held in her hands. They were religious to a man, and Jesper stared, mouth agape, he had never seen anything like it.

I lay in my bed that night and heard Jesper dreaming in his, he mumbled and tossed from side to side and suddenly he shouted out loud, and then he was quiet. I gazed at the picture of Lucifer. I could swear he had moved in the dark. And then I fell asleep.

During the days that followed there was more blood on the streets of Ålborg, there were strikes in Esbjerg in the town and the harbour and the Germans went amok. But the more people they beat and threatened, the more strikes were held and soon warehouses were ablaze, and there were fires in Odense and Kolding and many other places.

The German ship *Norden* lay at the bottom of Skagen harbour after an explosion that could be heard as far south as Ålbæk. The mine was a "limpet" with three magnets on each side that attached it to the hull and stayed firm even when the ship was at sea. Uncle Nils and two communists had made it on nightshift at the shipyard in our town, and it was Jesper who cycled to Skagen with the "limpet" on his luggage carrier and a Luger under his jacket. That was the longest ride of his life. It was a blazing hot day, but he could not even unbutton his jacket, and twice a German patrol drove past.

After a few days the *Norden* was salvaged from the mud and sent to our shipyard for repair, and it was not long before it was at the bottom of *our* harbour. Four workmen were arrested, but not Uncle Nils.

Two German soldiers came out of a house in Søndergade one morning and got into their car. They were heavy with sleep and bleary-eyed, they started up and were about to drive off, but the car did not move although they stepped on the accelerator and gunned the motor. They got out and saw the car had no wheels but rested on four piles of bricks. Then they savagely let fly with their sub-machine guns, now there were enemies all around them, and they broke all the windows in the block with their salvoes. An old lady was taken to hospital with a bullet in her thigh. She would personally hang every German with piano strings, she shouted.

We had been Hitler's little pet, but now it was *war*, and things would no longer be as they were in the verse we had learned:

> We speak French with the ladies
> and German with the dog,
> And Danish? That's for the servants.

The posters announcing "Man spricht Deutsch" disappeared from the shop windows. We did not do that any more. In one day almost the whole town suffered amnesia.

Every morning the milk lorry brought the delivery from the dairy, and my task was to stand at the door at six o'clock and wait till I heard the lorry coming, then go out and help the driver with the crates which were heavy, and listen to what he had to say that day in his oily voice about the mysteries of love, then take in the delivery and put the bottles in the cooling sink, knowing he was standing behind me staring up my legs when I bent over the icy cold edge. When he had driven off I rode the goods bike to the bus station where the ice machine was kept, remembering the two twenty-five øre pieces. I pulled the lever till the blocks of ice came sliding out and lifted them on to the bike with a gunny sack against the cold. Each time I lowered my face till I could feel the cold bite my cheeks, then blew out and saw the frost vapour float about in the late summer heat before I mounted the bike again and cycled back as fast as I could so the ice did not melt in the sun. In the shop I picked up the blocks and put them in place in the space on top of the icebox where they could slowly melt and run down on each side and keep everything cool inside.

There was enough milk, but most people were hard up. Many customers bought milk on credit and the Germans we delivered to paid in Kassenscheine instead of proper money, and those scraps weren't worth much more than toilet paper. But when my father went to the Commandant to protest he was met with curses for his pains.

So more and more fell on my shoulders in the shop, I had no other work. My mother set up her sewing machine in the living room and took commissions from the ladies of Rosevej. My father tried in vain to keep up the prices in the workshop, and Jesper worked on the newspaper.

I have put change in the till, I have cleaned and made room for new bottles in the cooling sink, for butter and cheese in the icebox. Now I am standing in the shop waiting by the open door without switching the light on. I like this early half-light, the mild air from the sea, standing inside looking out without being seen, and there are almost no sounds from the street, and I can think and remember who I am before anything new comes along. Everything happens so fast it's easy to forget, everything

139

is exploding and burning. But now it is quiet.

There's plenty of time before the milk lorry comes. I stand in the middle of the floor distanced from all things and think I will always remember myself like this, alone on the black and white tiles in the yellow blouse and the semi darkness, and I raise my arms and stretch them out and slowly turn my body around. I dance a dance so quiet only I can understand it, so as not to forget the body I have at this precise moment. I am seventeen, and my dance is so slow that nothing is lost of what is me up to this day.

I finish my dance and see myself from above and see myself from the side and take it all in, and it is still quiet as I go to the door and sit on the steps as the light spreads through the street, all golden on the top of the house where Herlov Bendiksen draws aside the curtain and looks out. A fishing boat starts up in the harbour, it beats little holes in the stillness. Jesper is doing the milk round today with the rest of yesterday's bottles. He will soon be back.

I look up past the roofs of the houses. There are two aeroplanes up there in the blue, so high they cannot be heard or identified. Perhaps they are English, perhaps there has been a drop in the night and an allied spy has fallen like an angel through the dark and sought shelter in a stable. Now he is lying in the hay looking out and waiting for the day in a ray of light for the last quiet minutes. Just like me.

Then I hear the car. It drones up Danmarksgade and it is coming from the north today and not from the south as usual; it turns the corner and comes down our street. But it is not the milk lorry, it is a car and it stops right in front of the shop. I get up from the steps and close the door and turn towards the street holding my hands clasped round the doorknob behind my back. Two men in uniform get out and one in a striped suit. This one is Gestapo Jørgensen. He is the man who chained Billegård the builder to a radiator and killed him with his bare hands in the Gestapo's house at Kragholmen. The whole town knows about that. Billegård was a friend of my father's at the Artisans' Union. When this war comes to an end Jørgensen is a dead man. The whole town knows that too.

Now he comes over to me and asks for Jesper.

"Is he up? Can we have a word with him?"

"He was up a long time ago," I say, "he's not at home."

"Where is he then?"

"He's gone to work."

Jørgensen looks at the clock. "So early?"

I shrug my shoulders.

"Anyone with an honest job has to get up early," I say. He doesn't like that. He looks daggers at me.

"Can we come in and see?"

"No."

"Out of the way," says Jørgensen. He pushes me aside, tears my hands from the doorknob and opens the door of the shop. My father has gone to his workshop, he is always early. Only my mother is upstairs. She is singing. She is in the kitchen washing up and clattering about, and the kitchen window faces the yard. The two soldiers

141

stay in the street, and Jørgensen walks in. His heels rap on the tiles straight through the dance that hangs there still in a shimmer he rips apart, and he walks towards the door of our room and pushes it open with one hand, holding his gun under his jacket with the other. He knows where Jesper sleeps, then he knows where I sleep too. Perhaps they've stood on the pavement looking in through the gap in the blackout curtain. Jørgensen bends down in the doorway and looks in. I go after him glancing sideways at the clock on the wall, and stand behind him. He turns round sneering.

"So this is where the love birds sleep. They only use one bed too. I might have known it." I look in, I have made my bed, Jesper hasn't made *his* as usual, and the way *he* tosses about at night makes it look as if two have slept in it. My face is burning. Jørgensen stares at my yellow blouse with its short sleeves and my brown arms and my breasts straining against the buttons, and he sneers again with moist eyes and I see what he sees, and I shout:

"That's not true!" I hate Gestapo Jørgensen, I want him dead. I hit out at his face, but he grabs my wrists and squeezes so hard I can feel them cracking, he can snuff out a life with those hands, and the pain makes the tears spurt out.

"You little wildcat! I don't care if you sleep with your brother, but I want to know where he is, do you understand!" He squeezes still harder, I feel sick, I'm going to be sick, I see the clock twisted into an eight on the wall, the second hand slams against the tiles, and I try to twist myself free and end up with my knees on the floor, looking up at his face that is big and raw as naked flesh. If only he would die now, his heart explode and his eyes fall out, and take with him everything they have seen and turned into hellish filth. If only Jesper could be delayed or get a puncture.

"He has gone to work, I tell you!"

"That's a lie!"

But it is no lie, for the milk round is work too, we take it in turns and he should be back by now and the German soldiers stand outside the window smoking and waiting and they will see him the moment he comes round the corner on the goods cycle.

I give up. I go loose in his grasp and let my forehead drop onto the tiles on the floor and start to cry. I am naked for all to see, and Jesper will be caught in a moment.

"Let go of her!"

Jørgensen starts, his arms jerk and I feel glad, he almost lets go of me and turns towards the door where Herlov Bendiksen stands on the steps with a soldier at each shoulder and says:

"She's telling the truth. He went to work half an hour ago."

"What's it got to do with you," says Jørgensen.

"Nothing. I'm just a neighbour, but I *saw* him go. So there's nothing for you here." He fills the doorway in his apron, with a smile on his face, he's a member of the Artisans Union. His forearms bulge in a cross over his chest. If the two soldiers had not been there Jørgensen would have been in trouble.

"I thought you might be interested."

Jørgensen slowly relaxes his grip, my arms flop down without blood or feeling. It is hard to get up, I cannot support myself with my hands, so I roll round and use my shoulder and knees, and my knees shake when I finally get up. I can feel I am still crying, my arms hang straight down, and I see Bendiksen's blue eyes holding Jørgensen in a vice. He fingers his lapel and finally turns towards the door to the staircase, almost unwillingly. He does not know what is behind *that* yet. I don't know either. He turns back to look at Bendiksen who moves back two steps so there's a free passage out to the street. He is still just as calm, his eyes just as blue, and Jørgensen starts to walk out. Halfway to the door he turns and snarls: "That bed won't keep you warm much longer, I can tell you!"

I wrench my body round and summoning all the strength in my half-dead arm I launch out at his face with my hand, but he easily parries and punches me on the cheek with the back of his hand so I fall backwards and land on the floor again. He has two rings with inset stones on that hand, they have pierced my face and I feel the warmth on my skin and the warmth of my blood starting to run. I close my eyes to the pain and stay there on the floor until Jørgensen has gone and I hear the car starting up in the street. Then Bendiksen helps me up.

"Are you crazy," he says, "he could have killed you. Why did you hit him?" But I do not answer.

"Where's Jesper?" I say. "He should be here by now."

"I know. Take it easy. The bike is in my backyard, he

borrowed another one. Do you think I don't know what's going on?"

But I know nothing about that. Since we have lived in Lodsgade we have only said "Good morning" and "Good evening" and "Nice weather today" or "What a downpour!" to each other, and I've no idea what he knows about me. But he *is* a member of the Artisans' Union and maybe he knows us through my father.

"Do you think I don't know the Gestapo car when I see it? One day I'll come across Jørgensen on his own in the harbour and then we'll be rid of him." He looks at me with that blue gaze like a child's, and I believe he means what he says. He strokes my hair and turns my head to the side.

"Perhaps you'd better wash off the worst of the blood before your mother comes down." I feel my cheek hurting again, and he is so safe and familiar and so new at the same time that I first bob, then lay my head against his chest and wipe the blood off on his apron, and he strokes my hair and says:

"Jesper told me to say you know where he is."

13

In one of the cold winters before the Germans came the ice lay shining all the way out to Hirsholmene. We stood on the hard-frozen shore with our skates tied in a string round our necks gazing out at the lighthouse, and it looked as if it was just a kilometre away across the water. Our breath hung in the clear air. Everything was at the same distance. Everything could be touched if we just stretched far enough. If we held our bare hands out straight we were sure to feel stones, ice, clouds, the roofs of Strandby and the frozen surf at Frydenstrand.

"I'm going across today," said Jesper.

We had been given screw-on skates for Christmas, my father had sharpened them in his workshop, and we used them every day for several weeks. There was hardly any snow, but the ground was frozen hard and the puddles and ponds were solid ice. The Elling brook was iced over as far as we had the energy to go. But now Jesper wanted to skate on the sea.

I hesitated. I knew the lighthouse was as far away as it always had been. It was tricking us, and I knew Jesper knew, but he could not resist it. The island with the lighthouse had always been there no matter where we stood on the coast looking out, and there was a school there, and twice a year the island children came from that school to our town in a fishing boat and walked through the streets bunched together in a little flock gazing at the shop windows. We talked to them and asked them questions and they knew a little about the world and a lot about the sea, but we had never been across to visit them.

Jesper sat down on an old fish box, he took the key from his pocket and screwed his skates tightly on to his boots. Ruben was there and Marianne, and Mogens who was a friend of Jesper's, and we all screwed our skates on tight and walked knock-kneed over the sand that squeaked horribly against the skates and on to the ice to test if it was firm. Jesper glided cautiously back and forth a few times, and when he felt it was safe he set his course straight out. Mogens followed him for some distance, but stopped where the third sandbank rose up slightly with crushed ice around it, then he turned and came back. I quickened my pace and did an aeroplane, I sailed off like my father on his bicycle with one leg straight out behind me and both arms to the side and ended in an almost successful pirouette, but it was not much fun because I had to keep turning round to look for Jesper's back that slowly grew smaller without the lighthouse getting bigger.

He was gone a long time. Marianne and Ruben had to go home, then Mogens went home, and I was left alone gazing out over the white sea waiting and waiting until the cold bit me so hard I could stand there no longer, and then I went home too.

A boy had fallen through the ice two days earlier and disappeared, but we did not know about that. The

147

grown-ups knew, and I had never seen my father so angry as when I arrived home alone that winter evening with my skates in one mitten and the other soaked in tears. Never again until several years later when I stood in the workshop with a big wound on my cheek, and my wrists swollen and blue from Gestapo Jørgensen's grip, and so bereft of feeling that when I tried to pick up a cup or a glass it fell to the floor at once and broke. My father stood before me in a frenzy with his hammer and chisel in his hands, and I was telling him what had happened, but only halfway through I suddenly realised he was furious because he was frightened and could not show it in any other way. That this was how it had always been, that I had always misunderstood. And then I knew too that he was never angry with me as he could be angry with Jesper. He hurled the chisel into the wall where it lodged quivering, and with the hammer he shattered the cupboard he was making until nothing was left of it but small bits and pieces. His back bulged and his forearms bulged with the effort and then he slung the hammer at the wall after the chisel so the chisel broke and both fell on the floor and lay there. He who could never end the day without hanging his tools up clean and tidy each in its place above the bench. Then he took off his apron and flung that on the floor too, pushed me out of the door and locked it.

I cycle north at dusk towards Kæret beach past the marshes at Rønnene where the seagulls sit in long rows in the shallows beyond the reeds, and all the rows take off as I ride past, unfold like grey-white sheets and land again in the dim light that slowly fades and disappears towards Skagen. There are thousands of them, I hear their soft rushing and feel the wind in my face as if this were the last time I would cycle here in just this way, and I see myself from the outside as more and more often I do, in a film at the Palace Theatre progressively one row of seats further back from the screen, on the same brown bicycle I have had for many years, and my hair streams back and at the same time almost merges with the advancing night, and I hear the creaking of my right pedal against the chain guard, squeak, squeak, again and again a thousand times, and my breath, puff, puff, quite alone with no other sound now the gulls are silent.

It grows darker and darker, but I do not light my lamp, for on these flat stretches I would be seen a kilometre away and the drone from the dynamo would block out all other sounds. I dare not do it. Everything would be easier on the road to Skagen further inland on the bridge over the Elling brook, but there is German traffic there now and it is past curfew time.

There is not a tree to be seen, only some low bushes that cannot grow any bigger because of the wind from the sea and the reeds in front of them in a dark wall against the last light. Far ahead where the road ends I steer the bike off the gravel, out into the marram grass and right down to the dunes by the shore. There I leave it at the end of the path where I know I shall find it again.

It is high tide. There is a dark shining mirror where

149

you can walk dryshod in the middle of the day, it covers everything and it is impossible to see which way the brook runs when it has left the reeds. I take my shoes off, put them beside the bike and wade out. The water comes up to my ankles, it is warm and pleasant and the bottom is soft on my soles. Little flounders have hidden themselves in the sand and they wriggle against my toes and shoot off when I put my feet down. If it had been light I could have followed the lines of whirling sand and caught them in my hands where the whirling stopped and felt them tickle my palms, put them in a bucket and watched them go flat on the bottom so as to be invisible.

I walk cautiously through the water, narrowing my eyes and peering for the darker current where the brook runs deeper, but everything is equally dark and smooth right out to the first sandbank where the waves roll in. I lift up my dress to be prepared but still I suddenly step into much deeper water than I had expected. I sink up to my hips at first and then to my chest, and I lose my balance and fall forwards until the water is up to my throat and covers the whole of my dress and thin jacket, and it is fresh water just here and much colder. I sob when I can't feel bottom under my feet, so I draw a deep breath and start swimming the few metres until I can reach bottom and the water only comes up to my ankles again.

The wound on my cheek smarts when I stand up, water pours from hair and dress, and the dress sticks close to my skin. It's like being touched by a hundred hands. I should have been less naked without clothes,

I think and pull off jacket and dress, and at once it is so lovely that I unclasp my bra and take off my pants and walk completely naked through the water, wringing out the clothes so it splashes around me and I can feel the big darkness close to my body. No one can see me, even the lighthouse is dark, and I am free from the eyes of Gestapo Jørgensen that have rested on me all day. But it does not take long for the gooseflesh to spread. It is autumn, and I can't remember when summer ended. Maybe today. Maybe yesterday. Maybe long ago. With a mirror I would have seen my skin grow slowly blue in big patches round my mouth, on shoulders and thighs. My teeth start to chatter. I cannot stop it, and it makes such a clatter I'm scared the Gestapo will hear it right in at Kragholmen. I put my dress on again and the thin cardigan, and it's not easy, I have to *drag* the sticky dress down over my hips, and that makes me even colder. And then I start to run. In over the shoals so water and wet sand splash around my feet until I get to the beach on the other side of the reed belt round the brook, and I run along the beach northwards as close to the water as possible so as not to step on the mussels and sharp shells lying in a white strip where they have been washed ashore a few metres inwards the whole way along, thinking that if only I run quickly enough the warmth of my body will *steam* the dress dry.

I didn't tell my father I knew where Jesper was, he was so angry I thought he might do something stupid, so he went to Uncle Nils in Søndergade to ask, but Uncle Nils was not at home. He was not at the shipyard either. He had vanished.

I stood at the corner of our street and saw my father coming back, he didn't turn down to the dairy shop, but went on walking to and fro on the pavement. He was so furious he couldn't talk, and people who knew him hurried past when they saw his face, and finally he stripped off his jacket, walked out into the road, flung it down on the cobbles and trod on it, and not until he picked it up again did he calm down. He shook it carefully as if asking forgiveness, put it on, and I went up to him and brushed the top of his back where he could not reach. Then he put his hand in his pocket and pulled out the few coins he had on him and looked at them, and I thought he was going to give them to me, but he turned and said:

"I'll be away an hour or so," and walked along the block and down Havnegade to the Vinkælderen.

For the rest of the day I stood behind the counter serving customers who came in, answering questions and smiling when they left, behaving as if nothing had happened when they stood there staring at my cheek. I had a cardigan on with long sleeves so the bruises should not show, and I concentrated and tried not to look down at the tiles or at the clock on the wall, and every time I picked up a bottle I used both hands in a way that looked natural. When five o'clock came I shut up shop and went upstairs for dinner stiff in every limb.

My mother had laid a place for Jesper. She sat biting

her lips not looking at his place. My father raised his eyes from his plate one single time and looked me straight in the face, and he asked why the hell I sat there smiling like that. He was probably a bit drunk, but my mother did not realise that, "but Magnus, really," she said, and I put my hand to my mouth and felt I had not taken off my smile for the customers yet. When I finally relaxed, my face hurt. At half past eight I changed into a clean dress and my knitted jacket and cycled out of town without saying where I was going, and now I am running along the beach in the dark as fast as I can with the sticky wet hem of my dress in one hand so as not to stumble over my own clothes and fall down.

Sometimes when I think of Jesper all I can see is his dark back on the way across the white sea to Hirsholmene. It gets smaller and smaller and I stand at the edge of the ice feeling empty. Why didn't he ask me to go with him? I have a will of my own, but if he had asked I wouldn't have hesitated. I always went with him. After all, I had to look after him and he had to look after me, and my father would have been furious with us both. Staying there alone was meaningless.

Sometimes I imagine he tells me everything, but I know that's not true. He never told me if he went all the way to Hirsholmene. I don't tell him everything either, but I feel he knows what I am thinking, and I know what *he* thinks. I have taught myself to do that.

And yet all the same I am not sure. I stop running when I realise I'm almost at the shack. Anyone could hear my breath, and I have to bend over and lean on my knees and pant down between my thighs until my lungs calm down and my heart stops beating so loudly I can't hear anything else.

He knew I would come. I straighten up and see a shadow a few metres away and I jump, but he says:

"Hi. I rather expected you earlier."

"It wasn't easy to get away, and I didn't want to start before it got dark." It is hard to talk, I'm still panting.

"That was good. Did you come along Skagensvejen?"

"There's German traffic on Skagensvejen, I took the coast road and then walked along the beach. No one saw me. I didn't meet a soul, only a crowd of seagulls. But maybe seagulls have souls. It's curfew now, after all."

"You had to cross the brook, then. It's deep there this time of day."

I start to laugh. "I know that," I say.

I can see him better now, his black hair, the dark shadows around his eyes, and he can see me.

"You're soaking wet," he says. "Come on."

He takes my hand and leads me through the darkness. His feet know the way so well he doesn't stumble even once though the path turns sharply and goes up and down, he goes first and I follow, it is like a dance through the marram grass and reeds until the still darker shack is right in front of us, and his hand is dry and warm around mine. He pulls the blanket aside, we bend down and go in. It is impossible to see anything. He lets go my hand and searches in the dark while I stand bent over waiting, my teeth chatter again, and then I hear the scrape of a match. It lights up and *Jesus lives* is embroidered over the window and on the wall hang Lenin and Jesper and me. I have not been here for four years. Everything is the same except for the paraffin lamp which is new. He takes off the glass and lights up, then he blows out the match and throws it on the sandy floor before putting the glass in place on the lamp again and adjusting the flame. He hangs a gunny sack over the embroidery in the window so no light can shine out and then he turns to me.

"Hey, you're bloody freezing, Sistermine. We must find you something dry."

"It's all right, I'm fine."

"Rubbish." He rummages in a heap in the corner and finds a woollen jumper and an old pair of trousers he has used for fishing.

"Sorry, this is all I've got."

"That'll do fine," I say.

The clothes smell faintly of fish and salt and Jesper. I do not know where to change. There is not much room in the little shack, the lamp lights up the whole of it, and I am wet right through. Jesper just sits there unthinking as usual, and it would be too silly to go out into the dark again. I don't want to anyway, so I turn my back and take off my jacket and pull the dress slowly over my head. I unfasten the bra and lay it all in a heap on the floor while I try to avoid Gestapo Jørgensen's gaze. I can't quite do it, I shut my eyes and then Jesper says quietly behind me:

"I've got to go to Sweden tonight."

I feel myself stiffen. Of course he must get away. He cannot stay in this shack long, he must have food and drink and someone must get it out to him. No one knows when the war will end, and as long as it lasts he must stay hidden. It's no good. Sooner or later he would be caught. But it had not occurred to me.

I have been standing bent over to hide my body, but now I straighten up and turn round slowly as calmly as I can, I have the jumper in my hand and I try to stop my teeth chattering. I am frightened and determined. He is squatting down looking at his shoes and then he raises his head and sees me in the light of the paraffin lamp. His face is quite clear and the flame of the lamp flickers in his eyes and I have to look past him to Lenin on the wall, but Jesper smiles and looks at me without saying anything and then he says:

"You're a good looker now, Sistermine."

"Gestapo Jørgensen says we sleep together."

I swallow, there is something in my throat I can't get down so I swallow again, but it does not help. Jesper just smiles.

"But we don't, do we."

"No," I say, and it is then he sees the wound on my face and the big blue marks on my arms. He gets up.

"Did Jørgensen do that?"

I do not reply. He takes the few steps towards me slightly bent under the roof, I swallow and drop the jumper.

"Bloody hell, the swine," says Jesper and raises his hand to touch the wound with his fingertips carefully. I lean my cheek against his palm, lightly at first and then harder and we stand there and he leans his forehead against my temple, his shirt just brushes my bare breasts, I meet him, I do not breathe, and he says:

"You're freezing."

"Yes."

"You're a sweet brave sister."

"Yes," I say.

He bends down carefully with my cheek in his hand and picks up the jumper.

"You're freezing," he says.

14

Jesper takes the photograph of the two of us from the wall and leaves Lenin hanging there.

"I'm taking this with me. If they ever find the shack they'll think it's the headquarters of the Communist Party. But *we* mustn't be seen in such company," he says, – "you in particular," and he puts out the flame of the paraffin lamp, and we bend down and go outside into the night and stand there until our eyes are accustomed to the dark, and then we start walking along the beach. He has the photograph in one hand and his shoes in the other. I carry my wet dress and jacket in a bundle under my arm. We walk the whole way without saying anything until we have to go into the shallow water before the reeds and the stream that runs out past the reeds, and it is still high tide. We roll up our trouser legs and wade. Jesper stops when we get near the stream outlet.

"It'd be pretty silly to get wet now," he says. "Wait here."

He wades off into the reeds, I hear splashing in there, but I can't see anything before there's a rustling again, and only then do I see his bare head faintly and he is standing in a rowboat poling his way out. It must have a flat bottom, for it's floating in the shallows.

"You didn't know about this, did you?" he says.

"No."

"It was on the wrong side, though. The owners will have to wade for it now. I've made use of it a lot."

He poles it right up to me, and I put the bundle of clothes into the boat and get in, and he pushes off with the oar and we glide over the brook until we scrape the bottom on the other side and then we jump out, and Jesper pulls the boat into the reeds and hides it there. We go on to the beach in the ankle-high water. It's darker than when I came. I cannot see farther than the back in front of me, but the water feels warm now, and I could go on for a long time in this way, just walking and walking and hearing the soft ripple of water around our ankles and never going in, but suddenly we are there. The sand is colder on the feet than the water was, it sticks to our wet feet when they sink into it, it irritates me, and I have to search until I find the bicycle. I'm quite cold even though I'm wearing the jumper, but I'm naked underneath.

"Here it is," I say aloud. Jesper follows my voice and comes up. I brush the worst of the sand off my feet before pushing them into my shoes.

"If you hold the picture for me you can sit behind me while I cycle," he says.

"Where's the bike *you* had?"

"Somewhere else."

He pushes the bike up the path and on to the road, I walk behind him. Once he stops and listens and we stand quite still.

"False alarm," he says.

When we're out on the road I roll up the dress and

jacket tightly and put the roll under the seat, then I sit on the luggage carrier with the photograph in one hand and the other on the seat, and when Jesper sits down I take my hand from the seat and hold on to the underneath of the bar so as not to touch him.

He hears the pedal rubbing against the chain guard right away.

"*That* won't do," he says, and I have to get off again. He lays the cycle down on the road and gives the chain guard a hard knock, and when we ride off the bike makes no sound. All I hear is the faint hum of the tyres on the gravel, I hold tight to the bar so as not to fall off, and I weep so quietly Jesper does not notice.

Near the Seaman's School we hear the sound of a motorcycle, and we see the light of its lamp so clearly that we have time to get off the road and in behind one of the big dog-rose bushes that grow so plentifully there. It's a German patrol, we see the motorbike go slowly past and the helmet of the man sitting in the side car and the blunt barrel of the sub-machine gun barely poking up.

We crouch down waiting till we are sure there are no more coming. Silence falls again.

"Did you actually get as far as Hirsholmen that time?" I ask, voicing my thoughts. He knows what I mean instantly.

"No."

"Was it too far?"

"Maybe. But what happened was that when I was halfway to the lighthouse I saw a cap lying on the ice all by itself with no one about. It really was a long way out

160

to sea, and the uncanny thing was that it was so like the one *I* had. It just lay there in all that whiteness and I didn't get past it even though I'd been determined to. I had to turn round, and I was frightened the whole way back. Much more frightened than I am now." He smiles and he does not look frightened, and I am not frightened either, just empty.

When we get near the harbour we dismount, and Jesper pushes the bike for a while before leaving it against the wall of an alleyway between two houses in Fiskerklyngen.

"You'll have to come and fetch it tomorrow," he says in a low voice. I put the photograph under my arm and leave my dress and jacket under the seat, and then we go down by the last houses before the north harbour where the gas lamps are dark along the road and there are blackout curtains in all the windows and no light anywhere even though we are almost into town. There has been a curfew after ten o'clock for three years, but this is the first time I've been out in the dark so late since the Germans came, and it gives me a weightless feeling, as if suddenly there is no meaning to anything.

We walk alongside the water from Fiskerklyngen to the little bay where the north arm of the breakwater starts with big boulders in rows on the outside facing the sea, and then the windbreak all the way, and behind the windbreak the footway goes along the harbour right out to the lighthouse. But the lighthouse isn't working and the boulders are in darkness and hard to balance on so I have to bend down and use my hands. It's not easy when I have to take care of the photograph at the same time, I'm afraid of stepping between two boulders, stumbling and breaking my leg. We have to go on the outside because there's a guard in a shed right in the harbour, and we won't get past him, says Jesper. He's right in front of me and whispers agonisingly quietly when he tells me how to move my feet. We are out of step, and there is a singing in my ears I cannot get rid of and I have to concentrate to hear what he says.

"Only twenty metres more now," he whispers. I nod, but he does not see that, and after a while he crawls up in the shelter of the windbreak and peers over the edge.

"Come on up," he whispers, waving. I crawl up and see what he sees. The harbour is still and dark. On the other side of the basin is the big house belonging to the rowing club where Jesper and some friends share a kayak. The building looks heavy and solid, and straight in front of us a pontoon sticks out. At the end of the short side a low speed boat is barely visible. I can see shadows moving in front of the boat and in the dark someone bends down to pick up something that might be a suitcase, but I cannot see who takes hold of it.

We climb over the windbreak and go down some stone steps and out on the pontoon. I am afraid the boards will creak in the silence. They don't, but the people standing there hear us at once and turn round, and a man growls – *Bloody hell!* half aloud, but Jesper raises his hand and then they recognise him. I don't know what I had expected, but when we get right up to them I see one of the men is Uncle Nils, and he says:

162

"You darned well made us jump, Jesper. We were only expecting one, you know." He doesn't look at me, he seems embarrassed.

"Sorry, I didn't think," Jesper says quietly. Uncle Nils turns to a man who looks like a fisherman, he has a blue woollen sweater and a cap of the same material, he is tall and angry, and Nils says:

"Everything in order," but the man doesn't look pleased. He doesn't look at me either, just stares at Jesper.

"Everything *is not* in order," he says. "Where did that girl come from?"

"She's my sister," says Jesper. His voice is submissive.

"Is *she* to go as well? I haven't heard anything about that!" I draw a louder breath than I intended, everything that was loose comes together again, the wound on my cheek pulses. They all turn towards me, Uncle Nils and the fisherman and what looks like a family. They come out from the shadows silently, and then I see it is Ruben and his parents and his sister, and Ruben smiles at me. But I do not care about him, I care about Jesper. I hold my breath and clench my fists. Jesper turns and looks at me as well, he tries a smile, but then he gets serious.

"No," he says, "no, she's not."

"I should think not," says the fisherman, mumbling something angry I don't understand and turning towards Jesper, but now I couldn't care less what he is angry about.

"Haven't you any luggage?" he asks.

"I didn't get as far as that," says Jesper.

"I've brought what he needs," Uncle Nils says, lifting a

big bag, carrying it to the edge of the pontoon and swinging it over to the man standing there. There's something familiar about that man.

"Well, that's all right, then," says the fisherman, "get them all on board now, and get on out. We can't stay *here* any longer. There'll be another patrol along soon."

Ruben and his family help each other on board, then Uncle Nils turns and looks at me for the first time and waves before he takes the hand of the man who has been standing waiting in the boat while we have been on the pontoon, and then he jumps óver.

"Come along, Jesper," says the fisherman, "your turn." But Jesper is standing staring at the man in the boat, and when he finally turns round he's wearing a happy grin.

"Well, kiss me till midnight. If it isn't Ernst Bremer! Sistermine, I'll be darned, it's Ernst Bremer!"

"Sure thing it's Ernst Bremer," says the fisherman, "on board with you now!" And Jesper comes over to me and puts his hand on my cheek. I let him.

"See you, Sistermine, it won't be long," he says and I say nothing and he goes quickly to the edge of the pontoon and hops on board.

Ernst Bremer starts up the engine at once, quite quietly at first like a faint hum and the boat turns till the bow points at the opening in the breakwater, it glides off in the dark until I can no longer see it. We stand waiting until it is safely out on the open sea, and then the motor rises to a roar, louder and louder and then fainter and fainter as it disappears right out to sea on its way to Sweden.

"No one can catch up with that boat now," says the

fisherman standing beside me on the pontoon.

"If you say so," I say. He turns in surprise and looks at my face, and then he looks at the jumper and the old fishing trousers and the photograph I still have under my arm that Jesper forgot in his delight at seeing Ernst Bremer, and he opens his mouth to say something, but closes it again. I just stand there. He strokes his face, and then he says:

"You can't go in through the harbour now. There's a guard right inside it and two in the harbour square. And besides, there'll be a patrol along soon. You live in Lodsgade, don't you?"

"Yes," I say.

"You'd better stay the night in my boat, then you can go in early tomorrow morning when the curfew's lifted."

"If you like," I say.

I still don't know the fisherman's name, or if he's still alive, but I slept with him that night in his boat. It gave me no pleasure, but he didn't say "No, thanks", and then *that* was done with. When Jesper came home almost two years had passed, the war was over, but by then I had already run away to Copenhagen.

III

15

I am twenty-two. He is thirty-six. He has curly red hair and seems shy, but he likes to talk. He talks about the Jotunheim and Valdres mountains. I don't know what I'm supposed to think about that. The shiny bus flashes past on Uelandsgate. It fills up the whole café window, I turn and look out, and he talks about eternal snow and ice and how beautiful it is with the whiteness right up to the sky and the strike of the valleys in between, and that it's possible to cycle there too, if you can find the right roads. He talks about Helge Ingstad. I don't get it, what is the strike of the valleys in between, and who is Helge Ingstad?

"I'm used to cycling," I say, " but not in the Jotunheim." He's pleased I'm Danish. It makes me different, and that's exciting. They've had nothing but Germans here for a long time; ein, zwei, drei, links – links. He's not very tall, but he's taller than me and seems younger than thirty-six, he's as eager as a boy, and his hands are hard and dry. I like that, I like his hands. He does all kinds of sport, boxing, long-distance running, football.

"Vålerenga is my team," he says, "Tippen Johansen, goal-keeper", and that must mean something, but I just look at him. I haven't got to know many people, it is not so easy. But I don't look too bad now, and I'm good at swimming.

"You can swim in the Bunnefjord," he says. "We have a cabin there, we built it ourselves."

"Who are we?" I say. He doesn't even smoke and he is not like anyone I met in Copenhagen or Stockholm. Maybe he's a bit too eager, a bit too shy. He blushes easily and after all he's thirty-six and probably has not had much experience. But he's not one of those who stand outside the door after work with a cigarette in one corner of their mouth barring the way and shouting:

"Here she comes, the Danish one!" I do not come. I go through the café and hop out of the kitchen window, past the dustbins towards the entrance and out on to the street where I can get the trolley bus to Carl Berners square. He doesn't tell dirty jokes.

I clear the table where he's sitting in an alcove, put his plate and cutlery on the tray and ask him if he would like anything else. He's had enough, but he wants to stay on, he wants a sweet.

"Caramel pudding," he says, smiling. I have to laugh. He looks so self-important. He puts both hands on the table and spreads his fingers. I look at his hands. A heavy lorry goes by, shaking the building.

"I can't really afford this," he says. He leans back, he's enjoying himself now, he has a powerful chest and his shirt is tight. It is so hot this summer, but his hands are still hard and dry.

"Afford to eat here every day, I mean," he says and that must mean something too, but I don't say what I ought to say, just go and fetch his sweet. I seem to do nothing but walk and walk. Some days I walk down Uelandsgate into town instead of taking the bus across it, and it's quiet in the streets in the evening, but hot too, and in such a grey town the house walls give off heat, the sun has just gone down behind the roofs, and I'm sweaty under the arms, in the groin, and I think it must be obvious. I should have had a bath, but there's not much room where I'm staying with Aunt Kari. My room is on the inside facing the courtyard and I can stay there as long as I work in the café. Aunt Kari is not my aunt, but my mother's, and she speaks in a mixture of Danish and Norwegian that is hard for everyone to understand. I only have a few things of my own in my room, some books I always keep with me and the four glasses I was most successful with at the glassblowing factory in Søder where I stayed with Uncle Peter in his weird house, and he is not my uncle, but my mother's. He had a stripey cat which stood on its hind legs and saluted like Hitler when Peter played the Swedish national anthem on the gramophone. I did not think it was funny, and we had an argument.

"You've no sense of humour," he said, "you take every-thing so seriously." That is not true, but no German soldiers had been standing about in Stockholm. It was a wild place, I liked it, but I could not stay there any longer, there were too many crazy people in the house, they hardly ever slept like other folk, and when Uncle Peter had money and wasn't blowing glass he was always drunk, and sometimes he forgot who I was and came into my room at night with his hair standing up and a haze before his eyes as thick as velvet. The first time I let him stay, and he wept and wept, but later on I didn't want to, and then I had to climb out of the window on to the fire-escape so as not to have to fight.

The café is known as Aunt Kari's,not its real name, we just call it that, and it *is* hers. Over the door it only says *Kafé* in gold on black glass. Nothing more. On each side of the sign is an advertisement for Blue Master Virginia cigarettes, we sell them at the counter, and the packet has a picture of a blue horse on it. It reminded me of Lucifer, and I bought a packet once, but they were stronger than the ones I was used to.

I walk down Hausmannsgate and catch myself thinking of his hands, but I'm sweating so much it turns out wrong when I think the thought right through, and then I need a bath again, so I turn down Torggata and walk the whole way from Ankertorget to Torggata Baths with my jacket over my arm and my arms held slightly out so they won't stick, but they do all the same. I hear my own steps on the pavement, a boy with grazed knees runs past and shouts out something I don't understand. Maybe it's something about me.

Almost every day I see him coming over Kiellands square from the Salomon Shoe Factory on the other side where he has been since he was fourteen, he tells me, and always at precisely quarter past five.

"This is the third time this week," he says, shaking his head as if he can't understand why he has fallen into such costly habits, but he'll soon be foreman and then everything will be much better. He wags his tail like a puppy, and I look at myself in the kitchen mirror when I carry out the trays and don't object to what I see when I look close enough. My mother was wrong, my long ringlets vanished in Copenhagen on the way from the Telephone Exchange to Vesterbro, but despite that the men stand at the door after closing time waiting with their essential patriot's hairstyle and their cigarettes.

I didn't mean to come here after Stockholm, I'd intended to go to London, but I did not have the money then, so I made my way up here to Aunt Kari to see a new town while I saved up for my ticket and waited for my documents. You need documents for everything now, it's 1947, and I should have had a letter from Jesper. I have not seen him for four years, but he knows where I am. He has gone to Morocco, and I have come to this town at the very end of the fjord where everything was grey and green on the way in on the boat, and then nothing but grey for days and weeks. There are still signs everywhere of those who left and it is hard to breathe when there is no wind. Only in the evening the dust and rubbish whirls in the gutters, and I sit by an open window in a bus going to Galgeberg, I know he lives near there. I walk down Vålerenggata past a big yellow wooden house with *First Ebenezer Congregation* on a sign on the ground floor, and I remember the Baptists next door in Asylgade and wonder, is this where my journey is to end? On the first floor a lady is standing at the window looking down on the street where I walk. Her hair is in a grey bun on her neck and she looks down with a commanding air.

The Queen of Ebenezer, I think, and I realise she is his mother, for this is where he lives and I can see him in her. She looks strong and perhaps beautiful, our eyes meet, and I am the one who looks away first.

I go further on before I stop, turn and take another way back past low houses with low fences. He is thirty-six and still lives at home with the two he calls mamma and papa. I take the bus right to the last stop on the other side of town and *walk* home. It takes me an hour and a half. I walk along the streets with my nose in the air looking for the horizon, but nowhere does the sky meet the sea or a plain, nowhere is there a line that is straight. Just grey hills around the whole town; you can climb them and buy a view for money.

A man laughs at my accent when I ask the way.

"Was German any better?" I ask. Every day the newspapers are full of cases against those who thought German was better. He blushes and points to the left.

"Past Salem, and then straight down," he says.

I say "thanks a million" in my broadest Danish and turn my back on him.

There are steps and columns at Torggata Baths and steps and columns at the Deichmanske Library. First I go to the baths and let a lady in white scrub me all over with soap till my skin is pink and shining in the lamplight. She tells jokes while she works and has hands like a carpenter's. I close my eyes and give myself over to her hands, it tickles in my stomach when I lean back, and she scrubs my front and says:

"Have you heard the one about the German soldier who missed the tram on 8th May, Liberation Day?" There's steam around me and her laughter is dark and soft, I smile without opening my eyes, I am sinking, and then I shower on the way to the pool and jump straight in and swim a thousand metres. Twenty times up and down without stopping, and I pay no attention to those who dive and jump and play in the water. I breathe as calmly as I can and swim with regular strokes among all the bodies, and then I go into the steam bath and sit on the bench until my head is as clean as my body and my thoughts rest in my skin. After yet another shower I go out and down the steps between the columns with a body that is heavy and light at the same time, and the city air strokes and tickles my neck. I go round the corner into Henrik Ibsensgate and walk up the street in the shade and further on up the slanting steps in the sun from Garborgs square to the square in front of the library and the steps up to it between the columns to the main entrance and then up the steps from the cloakroom to the loans section. Then I have to sit down. If I walk fast like that in the heat I shall have to go to the baths a second time, and I can't afford that. Twice a week is enough.

After an hour I come out with my arms full of the Golden Series. I read and read. I read a book a day; Anna Seghers, André Malraux, Ilya Ehrenburg, Hemingway. Last year we had the film of *For Whom the Bell Tolls*, and now it is in the library. I have to fight for it. A lady in a brown dress nearly hits me with her handbag when I take it from the shelf. She is red under her powder and sweating under her arms, and she pushes up her sleeves when she rages towards me.

"I should have had that!"

"Come back in a few days," I say, but that is not good enough for her.

"You're not even Norwegian," she snarls, following me round among the shelves, ranting and raging so loudly that everyone in the library turns and stares in exasperation. The man in coat and hat by the end shelf stamps on the floor and mumbles *bloody females*. I retreat to the desk. The woman behind it is the same one as before, she knows me and looks me straight in the face saying:

"You won. But there *is* a waiting list. That book shouldn't even have been on the shelf. But I know you read quickly." Then she winks, puts her hand to her mouth and turns her back. Her shoulders shake, and I laugh the whole way down the steps and ask a friendly-looking man the way to the nearest kaffistove.

"I'm sorry. I don't speak Norwegian. I'm new here, you see. Arrived only yesterday. From London."

"Oh. What I did was I asked you for directions to the nearest kaffistove, but then you wouldn't know."

"No, I wouldn't. What's a kaffistove, by the way? It sounds like an oven of some sort."

"It's a café. For people from the countryside."

"You're from the country, then?"

"Yes, but not from this one." I smile, he looks at me, bewildered, and I say:

"I'm Danish. So I'm from another country."

"Oh, I see. Very funny. So am I then. From the country,

but not from this one. Oh well, a kaffistove sounds good to me. May I buy you a cup of coffee, if we find one?"

"You certainly may," I say, laughing, and he likes it when I laugh, that's what he says anyway.

We go to Bondeheimen, the Farmer's Rest, I've known where it is the whole time, and we have coffee there and speak English. I thought it would be difficult, but when I open my mouth it just pours out. Everything I have read queues up to be spoken. He is a good listener, and when he finally asks me back to his hotel room, I feel badly about it and say yes.

I wake up, and it's still day. There is light on my eyelids and light in the room when I open my eyes. The window is wide open. I hear a tram in the street, and realise it is not my room. There is a chandelier hanging from the ceiling with chains of cut- glass pieces meant to look like crystal. I must have fallen asleep, but I do not remember when. Maybe straight away. That would have been something. I roll round under the bedclothes. He is sitting naked on the edge of the bed leafing through my books. I don't like him. I don't like his back. I have changed my mind. I don't want to go to London after all.

"You're a communist," he says without turning round.

"Of course I am," I say, "we're all communists here. Take your hands off my books."

"My suspicions exactly, this place is crawling with communists," he says; but I am not a communist, I don't know any communists. Jesper may be a communist, but I do not think so. Uncle Peter is not a communist either,

177

177

but in his house there were sometimes long lunches when ten or maybe fifteen lodgers debated for hours. The sixty-year-old man who is not my uncle, but my mother's, sat hungover with his ruined lungs at the head of the table, more of a chairman than a landlord, and what they were discussing was the Spanish Civil War and not the big one that had just ended. Johannes with a shade over one eye had stood in the streets of Barcelona feeling the stench of fouled powder from discarded rifles tear at his nose, and he felt the same in his sleep ten years later. In his dreams he heard the screams of his comrades, and the communists were not popular at that table. They had betrayed the Catalonian syndicalists and shot them in the back in the hour of destiny.

I usually sat listening, and a lot of what was said was meant for me. I was a woman and young, and they grew red in the face and excited, with their hands in the air competing for who would come out with the most brilliant riposte. Those elderly men infected me with their enthusiasm, they did not speak in one voice, they interrupted each other and dressed up history in words and flickering yellow-brown pictures until it felt like a home, and I was the guest of honour. They took me to a momentous event in Folkets Hus at Klara to hear the young author and editor Stig Dagerman presenting his views on anarchism. His was the new voice in their choir and the hope of the future until late one night when he went into the garage beside his house, closed the doors and ventilators and ran the car engine at full throttle.

But at Klara he was only two years older than I was and had six more years to live. I sat in the hall listening to everything he said with his sad eyes and childlike smile, and when the meeting ended Uncle Peter took me by the hand and led me up through the rows of chairs to the podium to meet him. He came down from the lectern with his briefcase under his arm, and his hand was no bigger than mine. We sat there talking about horses. He described the brown one they had on the farm where he grew up. It could take off his grandfather's hat to get at the sugar lump on his head underneath it and put the hat on again, and I told him about Lucifer who vanished into thin air after *my* grandfather had hanged himself in the byre. He wanted to use that story in a book sometime, if I would give him permission. I did.

When he picked up his briefcase to leave, he said:

"Hasta luega, compañera," and I said:

"No pasaran," which was the only thing I could say in Spanish and saluted with clenched fist as was Jesper's habit. It may have been the wrong thing to do, but he smiled and did the same and turned to go out of the door.

But in Oslo I don't know any syndicalists. The naked Englishman sits on the edge of the bed leafing through my books. He lays a finger on the name Ilya Ehrenburg and says I am a communist, and that's fine with me. I'll gladly be a communist to him. I go across the room naked to fetch my clothes and put them on slowly, garment after garment. He turns and gazes, but I go on as

179

if he were nothing, and he is left alone with his ridiculous white body.

"My books, please," I say, and he hands me the whole pile, and I put them under my arm and walk out of the room and down the stairs to the reception.

I walk and walk, smell the dust on the edge of the pavements and the house walls and the indefinable dampness from the river that runs through the town and the sour sweetness from Schou's Brewery where the great copper boilers tower, shining on the inside when I go past and where there is always someone standing shading their eyes with their hands gazing in through the windows. I walk down Trondhjemsveien in the evening to save the cost of the bus fare and use the money on the cinema instead, I go to everything that's on. I sit in the dark of a full house, evening after evening, staring at the screen, feature films, news films, documentary films, cartoons, I watch Tom and Jerry, and a lady in the sixth row can't stop laughing. She goes on after everyone else has stopped, they all turn round in the dark to look at her but she cannot stop. She can't have laughed for a long time, she starts to feel ill and has to be carried out, the light streams in from the door at the back and goes out again, and we hear her weeping and laughing on the other side and shouting:

"No, no. I don't want to."

I don't want to either. I get up and excuse myself to flickering faces, and everyone has to stand up the whole way along the row so I can get by. I go out past the box office and right out to the street where the evening is still light and the shadows lengthening, and the low sun shines straight at me on my way up Karl Johansgate. There are no familiar faces anywhere, and I think, why doesn't Jesper write me a letter. I get a letter from my mother once a month, and she writes: "If you have the light on your brow and Jesus in your heart, good fortune will go with you." Along Studenterlunden I have the light straight in my eyes, but Jesus deserted me a long time ago.

16

There is a letter for me forwarded from Denmark. From Helga in Magdeburg. The postmark tells me it has taken several months to get here. The last time I heard from her was in the summer of 1939, and I sent a reply. We were to meet, we said, but then came five years of bombs and flames and two years of silence, and now she lives in the Russian-occupied zone and doesn't go out. The soldiers march about the streets singing, and her dog Kantor howls.

It is a long time since I have felt like thinking of her.

I read the letter in my room with the window open on to the courtyard. It is evening, the air does not move, nothing moves except the pages each time I put one down on the bed. It is a long letter full of bitter words. Walter died at Stalingrad, her father died of grief, and then a long list of things they cannot get, which they thought they would find now it is three years since the war ended, and I wish I could feel sorry for her. To her the war was a tidal wave that came and went, and no one could do anything about it, and the shame she does in fact feel makes her angry. Now at least everything should be as it was before. But nothing is as before. They live in a cellar with the four-storey house in ruins above them, it is still winter, the water runs down the walls and they have a coal fire that is just as damp, it smokes and spreads soot over everything. I do look awful, she writes.

I drop the last page on to the bed in irritation and just sit there.

"Aren't you feeling well, my dear?" asks Aunt Kari. She stands in my doorway with her black silk dressing gown round her odd body. She is fifty-nine and almost as broad as she is tall, and it is her heart that takes up so much room. She has a dark shadow of moustache over her lips that are always red and curlers in her hair that is unnaturally dark.

I tidy the pages into a pile and look at her.

"Why do you ask?"

"Take a look at yourself in the mirror, my girl."

But I do not. Dear Helga, I write, this is probably not the right moment, your before is not like my before, I write, but I do not send it.

He is persevering. He is on night shift from Friday to Saturday and he comes across the square in the light under the trees just before opening time and stands there in front of the door with hands in pockets waiting till I let him in. He wants breakfast. This is new. I am under increasing siege. His eyes are red from lack of sleep and he is not so supple as when he steps out among the tables to show the basic movements in skiing or dances around with invisible boxing gloves on, one fist before his face, and the other whirling around my head or Aunt Kari's, and then suddenly blushes, smiles shyly and goes back to his place.

Now he sits in the alcove nearest the window and says:

"Excuse me a moment," puts his arms on the table and his head on his arms and stays like that for at least ten minutes before he straightens his back and orders rolls and coffee. He suffers a little for appearance's sake, for my sake. That is sweet, but not impressive.

At the Central Telephone Exchange in Copenhagen I worked double shifts many times and sometimes three in a row, to earn a bit extra, and then I took pep pills that Luise got for me, she had started work there the same day as I had. We teamed up and shared a flat in Vesterbro, and I do not know what was in those pills, she got them from a doctor she knew, but we could keep on working for two days and nights without sleep, and then we flopped into bed and slept for twenty-four hours. When we woke up we were empty-headed with no memory, and a hollow feeling in the body that made our legs shake, and we could hardly put on our dressing gowns and stagger out into Istedgade to the bakery on the next corner to buy bread and milk. We sat on the front steps eating breakfast there in our dressing gowns before we could get ourselves up the stairs again.

And then it was back to work. When the weekend came the extra earnings went on the flicks and the switchback railway at Bakken amusement park outside town. We rode and rode until our spines were like jelly, and we shrieked and screamed until our voices gave up and our stomachs turned themselves inside out. When the gondola finally stopped, we stumbled out and ran round the bushes behind the big framework to the fence, and there we leaned our foreheads against the wire netting and vomited spun sugar and baked apples until our stomachs were quiet again, and then Luise started to laugh and then I laughed, and we wiped our mouths and got out the last of our money and had one more ride. We were two girls from the provinces who screamed the evenings away and could never get enough.

The days and weeks with Luise went by in one stream, *at* work and after work, in the dark streets at night and the dark cinemas, in the flickering light of the screen where Cary Grant never stopped talking and in the light on the wet asphalt of Kongens Nytorv on humming bicycle wheels along phosphorous tramlines, to and fro, to and fro, on fixed routes. And I liked my work despite the military organisation with head duty manager and duty manager and duty sub-manager and strict supervision of clothes and language. I felt I was good at German and English and would soon be moved over to international where more help was needed, and I wanted that, so I never refused overtime when I was asked. And I was asked more and more often. I did late shift one day and double shift the next. Luise gave me a pill before I went downstairs in the morning and got out my bike and bowled along Istedgade and through the King's Town in pouring rain on my way to the telephone exchange among thousands of other cyclists. Not until late in the evening did I look up at the big clock on the wall, and then it was always ten, and there was another hour before I could get home to bed.

But it was too much in the end. It was the third week of three double shifts at a stretch. I knew I was tired, but I did not feel it. What I felt was a sensation round my eyes as if the skin was cardboard, and I heard a buzzing that irritated me, and I thought it came from bad telephone lines, but when I took off my earphones it did not go away. The voices I heard came from the bottom of tin buckets, and even though I understood what everyone said and answered all the questions correctly and connected the right wire to the right line, I had forgotten everything the next moment. A light came on again, I plugged in, and a blurred voice said:

"Can I speak to my wife?"

"Does she work here?"

"Are you suggesting *my* wife works at the telephone exchange?"

"Well, I don't know, do I, it was you who asked for your wife."

"Tell me something, young lady, are you being impertinent?"

He'd certainly had a few, that was obvious, and it had not done his temper any good.

"No, not at all."

"That's good. I can hear you are from North Jutland. I have had a lot of unpleasant experiences of North Jutlanders, I can tell you. So now you will just set up a conversation for me with my wife without further ado."

He speaks slowly and *very* clearly as drunk men do when they want to show they are not drunk, and I felt I wanted to get home, that I had no more to give.

"As to where I come from that's nothing to do with you, and as to your wife I haven't the slightest idea who she is or where she might be, so it will be pretty difficult to connect you. If you had helped me along a little it would have been fine."

"Tell me one thing, young lady, don't you know who my wife *is*?"

"It's a pity to have to admit it, but I don't."

"And you don't know who *I* am either?"

"Haven't a clue. But you've obviously had a couple of schnaps too many, so now I think you should go and lie down. Take a big glass of water and two aspirins on your way to bed. That's my advice. Goodbye."

I disconnected him, and that was that. It was five to eleven, so I shut down my position and went home to sleep like a stone until far into the next day when I was due on late shift. I ate my lunch standing at the worktop still asleep and cycled the whole way to the exchange with my body full of dreams, and in the corridor I met Luise on her way out from early duty. She looked at me with big eyes.

"You're to go to the duty manager at once. They're completely hysterical in there."

"What's it about?" I said, and she threw out her arms.

"I would have thought *you* knew that, but whatever it's about, it's something outrageous."

I went in through the switchboards looking at the ceiling, the voices dropped and there was silence in the big hall, the only thing I heard was my own footsteps on the floor. My shoes were new and rather expensive, and now I had no more money for the rest of the month. At the duty manager's office on the other side I looked in through the glass door, and saw her standing there stiffly behind the desk with two stripes on her sleeves, and out on the floor stood a man in a grey coat and one in a grey suit. That was the director, I knew, for he always greeted people with his whole body and smiled with glossy eyes at every female under twenty-five.

I knocked and went in, closing the door behind me.

What they said was that the drunk man who wanted to talk to his wife the night before was the King. The King of Denmark. They did *not* say he had been drunk. I had been insolent to the King of Denmark, and since there was still a week left of my probationary period of six months, I was dismissed as from today. They didn't ask me for my version, and I didn't ask them to listen to it either, because if I have to ask for something, I no longer want it.

"How did they know it was you?" said Luise.

"I'm the only North Jutlander in the whole telephone exchange. The King is has nothing but bad experiences of people from that part of the country."

I borrowed some money from Luise and travelled to Stockholm to become an apprentice glassblower with the Danish immigrant Peter Aaen in the working-class district of Søder, and I tell all this to the man in the alcove nearest the window on to Uelandsgate, that I was kicked out of the central telephone exchange in Copenhagen because I had been impertinent to the King of Denmark.

**

He grows thoughtful. No one in his family has ever been fired from a job. They have turned up faithfully at the factory every single morning at six or seven o'clock, his father, his brothers, year in and year out, and he says he has only stayed away from work one single time when he had to go to hospital with a back he had ruined ski jumping.

"It's not healed yet," he says. "When it gets too bad I have to wear a corset. As tight as hell."

And they have a different way of thinking about the King here than we have in Denmark. No one offends the King of Norway and makes jokes of it next day even though the King is Danish, and I didn't tell it to make a joke either. But it's given him something to ponder about as he takes the bus in from Waldemar Thranes gate instead of relaying the latest news from the boxing ring or the old boys' team at Vålerenga where he still plays football twice a week.

The café shuts early on Saturday. It is a restaurant, not a place where you can sit over beer after beer until late at night and talk till you're thick in the head.

"Off you go, then," says Aunt Kari. "It's Saturday. I have to make up the till and close up. You're going into town, I expect?"

It's not called town here on Kiellands square though it is part of Oslo. The town is the centre.

"I don't know."

"Oh, surely," she says, but I stand there while she does

the books and puts the money from the till into a little leather bag.

"I don't know," I mumble again, feeling as heavy as the mattresses I have seen out in the rain in autumn, impossible to budge, heavy as a dead animal. I rub my eyes, and she walks round putting out the lights, and I go reluctantly out of the door and wait on the pavement until she comes out and locks up with one of the keys in the big bunch she always keeps in her coat pocket. It's blowing hard down the street, I look around for a way to go.

"Well?" says Aunt Kari.

"Do you never feel homesick?" I ask.

"Home," she says, "where's that?"

"Aren't you happy here?"

"Not for one second."

"But you could have gone back, surely. Why didn't you?"

"L'amour," says Aunt Kari, "and now it's been too late for long time. There's nothing to be done about that."

She suddenly turns and walks towards her car and throws the money bag through the half open window on the driver's side, opens the door and gets in. She is the only woman I know who can drive a car, a black Citröen from before the war. When I ask where it came from she replies:

"It was just left lying about."

"Have a good Saturday in town," she says through the window, starts the car and turns out from the kerb. I stand there watching her drive across Kiellands square

190

and along Sannergate towards Carl Berners square before I turn and start to walk down.

But I don't go right down to the centre. Just past Telthusbakken I turn and take the road through Fredensborg to the Deichmanske library from the back, past the Swedish Margareta Church. I shouldn't have left Stockholm. Those old men were not so bad. They were exhausting, but they slept far into the morning dreaming of Barcelona, and I went down to the glassblowing factory on the ground floor, and it was quiet there then and there was light on the dark window from the lamps in the ceiling and light and heat from the flames in the furnace. It shone on Uncle Peter's glistening forehead when he coughed and bent over the long blowing pipe and did not want to look at me because he had been drunk the night before and had stood outside my door calling out a name that was not mine until far into the night. I should not have taken the train to Gothenburg and the boat across the sea to Denmark, should not have stood on deck through the opening in the breakwater with the old lighthouses flashing and flashing at our town where Pikkerbakken was lost in fog behind the houses and Frydenstrand Hotel in darkness to the north and only one drunk stood on the quay vomiting, wisps of fog around his legs. I should not have put my suitcase into the room behind the dairy shop only to leave again a week later. I had not been there for two years, and my mother was at my heels up the stairs asking questions about everything she could think of; why I had gone away as soon as the Germans left, *before* Jesper came home, why I didn't stay in Copenhagen, in Stockholm, why I did not write home.

Jesper was not there when the boat arrived. There were none of his things in the bedroom. Greta Garbo had gone and the red curtain and Rosa Luxemburg who had hung on the wall throughout the war camouflaged as an aunt of my father's, she had gone too.

"Where is Jesper?" I asked.

"Jesper is in Morocco," my mother said harshly, "but perhaps you have had enough of the world." I could not recognise her. I stood beside the old bed where Lucifer still hung on the wall. I took garment after garment out of the suitcase. She stood in the doorway with her hands crossed over her chest, and I thought she looked ugly. Her skull pushed at the skin of her face, her eyes were a bottomless blue, I looked through them.

"There's plenty to do *here*," she said. Then I slammed down the lid, left the rest of the things and went out.

It was nearly dark and there was no curfew. I walked the streets for several hours, up Danmarksgade and down again, out on the quay and back again, and all the way north to Rosevej. Lone's house seemed further away from the road than before, no light in any window, the fence was broken in several places, and the hedge had grown to a gigantic height. The nameplate on the gate had been taken down. It had never been painted underneath, and I stood gazing at the grey square. I passed my fingers over it. The wood felt rotten and decaying.

One day I saw Ruben in the town. He walked straight past me in the street, but he didn't know me. Maybe because of my short hair. For a moment I thought I might seduce him shamelessly, take him into Vannverks forest or out to Kæret beach among the dunes. He would be naked and speechless in the wind, and he would see who I was. But his back grew smaller on his way along the pavement, and I stood there without waving or calling him. He was alive anyway. Almost all the Jews in Denmark got away in time on board speedboats, fishing boats and rowing boats, thanks to people like Jesper. But Jesper was in Morocco, and I couldn't stay at home, the breakwater arms were crushing me, there was a paralysis in my body, my limbs were stiff and my lips dry, I could not breathe, could not speak, and I wanted to go to London but only had enough money for Oslo.

Six silent days in Lodsgade, and on the seventh I put my clothes back in my suitcase and went down to the boat. My father went with me. He wanted to carry the case. It was ridiculously light, but I let him do it and walked a few steps ahead so he could not see my face. He said nothing on the way down and nothing when I went up the gangway of the old boat. The *Melchior* was still in service.

Once on the boat I put my case in the cloakroom and went up on deck to the after rail. He stood by himself a few metres from a group of people shouting and waving handkerchiefs, and I thought he might be going to wave too, but he did not, just stood there in the long coat he still wore when it was windy, with his hands at his back and his brown beret on his head, and it was not possible to see what he was thinking, his face was perfectly calm.

The engines were started, the hawsers let slip from the bollards on the quay and smacked down into the water before the winches pulled them on board, and the deck vibrated. Then my father raised his hand and took a cigar out of the waistcoat pocket under his coat, lit it and blew the smoke out into the wind. The smoke blew back in his face, and I knew it smarted, that the tears rolled down, and I squeezed my eyes into narrow slits and looked down on to the quay and my father through a swirling mist. It was irritating, I blinked hard, but could no longer make him out.

17

It is autumn. Jesper and I play on the slope above the old well. We have to cross a field behind the Chinese garden to get to it. It is not cold enough yet to have to wear shoes. The corn has been cut and the fields are open. We are free, we can go where we like, and there is no one to scold us. The sky is high, we can run without getting wet through. It is a good place to play, sheltered from the wind and no one can see us, it's just Jesper and me. Far away we hear an axe in the forest and the horses at Vrangbæk and Grandfather shouting, but he isn't shouting at us. There is quiet around us. We can play. We run after each other on the slope that's round as a crater, in the middle is the open well, and there is thick grass there that is good to run on. I am trying to catch Jesper, but it's not easy. He is quick, he is Ernst Bremer and I am a customs man, and no one can catch Ernst Bremer. We run in a circle until the sky spins round and we get dizzy and totter in zigzags and we are drunk farmers. We have seen drunk farmers lots of times. Grandfather gets roaring drunk once a month but Jesper is even drunker, he staggers and clutches his head crying:

"Oooh, I feel so bad!" and he bends down to be sick, and he is. He makes rattling noises in his throat. Never has anyone been as drunk as he is. He holds on to his beard like Grandfather does so as not to mess it, and his head is heavy and hurting.

"Oooh!" cries Jesper, "I feel so bad, I want to die!" I shudder with joy. No one can mimic as well as Jesper, he's the only one who dares. He tilts forward, he falls, he holds on to his ankles so he turns into a wheel and rolls downhill to land in the well. I laugh aloud. There is a splash, and first he disappears and then he comes up again, but not his head. His round back hits the surface, he's still holding his ankles and floating like a ball with his head under water. And then he sinks again. The old well is so big that you have to swim a few strokes to get ashore. I can't swim yet, it's Jesper who can, but he does not let go of his ankles.

"JESPER!" I cry, and he comes up again back first. I kneel at the edge and stretch out my arm, but I cannot reach him. Then I start to run. Up the slope and across the fields to Vrangbæk. I run as fast as I can over the stubble on bare feet, and it really hurts at first and then not so much, and I run still faster. I've heard you're dead when you go under the third time. I have to hurry. The wind has dropped. The whole world is quiet, the sky above the farm and the yellow trees in the garden and the hill up towards Gærum where the cows graze, and the calves in the paddock stand still staring, they aren't chewing, the smoke from the chimneys doesn't move, and it's a long way to the farm, much further than before. I don't understand it. I summon all my strength, the pain in my feet has gone now and suddenly everything eases, I take off, I fly, it's the only right thing. At last I come to the first trees. I run through them and across the bridges in the garden straight on to the farmyard, and stop on the cobbles. There is Grandfather. I can't talk, I point back the way I have come. He turns and looks that way and shakes his head. I pull at the sleeve of his jacket but he gets hold of me round the waist and picks me up. He shows me my feet. My soles are nothing but blood and shreds of skin. There are red tracks on the cobbles behind us. I feel ashamed, I want to get down, we must go to Jesper quickly. I struggle in his arms but he holds me firmly and starts to walk towards the steps of the house. Then I see Jesper come into the yard, water streaming from his clothes, and he's laughing.

It is September and suddenly there is autumn around me, the sky high above the houses at Fredensborg, it's been cold for a few nights and this is the first chilly day. I'm freezing in my light clothes, I shiver so much my teeth chatter and I hurry along the road to Deichman. A rag-and-bottle man drives straight towards me with his horse and cart shouting:

"Any old bottles and rags!" up at the windows on both sides of the road, "Any old bottles and rags!" and from one or two houses ladies with head scarves and tremendous forearms come down to the gateway dragging bundles, put them on the pavement and stand waiting with their hands at their sides and their heads cocked and eyes like narrow slits. They look fearsome, but the rag-and-bone man smiles. He's been expecting this, he knows them, he cracks his whip over the horse and is lord of the street. The old horse starts and stumbles, the man shouts at it and cracks the whip again, but the horse can't manage to stand upright, its forelegs give way, its whole body sags, and it collapses on to the ground, the shafts bend and the cart slowly tips, I hold my breath, and the man jumps off the seat swearing loudly. The frayed edges of his jacket flap. Rags and bottles slide down off the cart and the bottles break and fragments of glass fly up and spread to all sides.

"You bleeding brute!" shouts the rag-and-bone man, "god-damned good-for-nothing nag!" he screams, raising the whip, he runs at the horse and thrashes it soundly to make it stand up. But it does not stand up, just struggles to breathe so loudly above the sound of breaking glass that I can hear it right over where I'm standing, and the ladies hear it at their gate. Now their eyes are round, their hands hang straight down, and I run up and seize the man by the arm with one hand and tear the whip from him with the other and jab him in the chest. He tumbles backwards, and I hit him with the butt end of the whip on the thigh, I hit him again as hard as I can and hold on to the whip with both hands.

"Are you daft?" he yells, clenching his fists, but he's afraid of me and opens them again to feel his thigh, and then I hit him on the hand. He howls, a red weal comes up on the back of his hand and beads of blood appear on the weal. I throw down the whip and bend over the horse, put my cheek to its neck, feel the cold against my knees and the warmth of the big body on my jacket and stomach, and the only sound in the world is the painful breathing against my ear. I close my eyes, I'm tired, I could fall asleep now. The horse fights to breathe. And then stops. I open my eyes. It is dead. It just died, and at first all is quiet and then I hear running in the street.

"Is 'e dead?" says one of the ladies from the gateway. I blink, I can see my reflection in the horse's eyes.

"I am afraid so," I say.

"You're Danish," she asks, but it isn't a question. I get up, brush dirt from the front of my skirt and pull my jacket close around me.

The rag-and-bottle man sucks the blood from his hand. "Is 'e dead?" he says, "e's not dead, 'e's the only one I've got. D'you realise that, you Danish maniac. 'E's all I've got!"

"Then you haven't got anything now," I say.

I turn and walk off. I feel their eyes on my back. The wind has got up, the narrow street is like a funnel that sucks in all the air and sends it out at the other end. The wind thumps me on the back, and in front of the steps of Deichman it comes from several directions, up all the streets from the fjord, through all the alleyways and makes free with the square, a labyrinth of wind, and the only escape is to go inside. I hurry up the steps, but halfway to the top I see it's too late. It's closed. I stop. The staff come out of the big door, it's Saturday, they laugh and chat, and in the centre of the group is the woman behind the desk I always go to. She sees me at once and smiles, I do not smile back, but despite that she stops at my step and says:

"It can't be *that* bad, it's only one day, and then we're

open again. Haven't you anything to read?"

"Oh, yes," I say. I'm shaking and don't want her to notice.

"But you're quite white in the face. You're not wearing enough clothes. It's really cold today. Where were you thinking of going?"

I shrug. Nowhere. I was not going anywhere.

"You can come home with me, I live quite close by," she says and points the way I've come from, but I do not move. She puts her arm around my shoulders.

"Come along, you must get thawed out," she says, hugging me. I stand quite still, I wait, I lean against her, and slowly I feel warmth come out from under her coat. I listen to her breathing. I don't want to walk, I want to stand there for a bit, and we do, and then we go.

The horse has gone from the street I came from, the cart has gone, and there are no ladies standing in the entrance to any courtyard. I stop and look around me, I must have been dreaming, I must have fainted or something is wrong with my brain and I am seeing things that do not exist. But there are fragments of glass on the pavement. Someone has removed the worst of them and swept the rest to the side. Someone has removed a whole horse and a cart full of bottles and rags.

"Now he hasn't got anything," I say.

"Who?"

"A man who had a horse. It is dead now."

We go past a block and round the corner to Rosteds-gate and into an entrance where the stairs are paved with tiles in a pattern of stars on each step, blue and grey and pink, and rails of wrought iron at the sides. All the staircases in Oslo have wrought iron rails. "Solgunn Skaug" reads a sign on her door on the first floor. The corridor is painted blue and there are books and pictures in her living room, but they are not like the ones in Lone's house. Here there are piles of books on the floor from the overflowing shelves, and the pictures are photographs.

"My family," she says, pointing. "Keep your jacket on, we'll warm the place up first." There's a stove in the corner. Solgunn fetches wood from a box in the corridor and an old newspaper. I go round looking at the books, I have read many of them. She bends down in front of the door of the stove, crushes paper and puts it in through the open door and lights it, then stays crouched down until she hears the wood crackling. She has fair hair, it is very smooth and cut straight below her ears so her neck is bare when she bends forward. It is very white. We stay near the stove with our hands held out in front of us waiting for the heat. I hear the wind beating at the window. I hear the clop of horseshoes in the street.

"Perhaps it's still alive," says Solgunn.

I shake my head. She takes off her coat and hangs it in the corridor and I take off my jacket. A desk is like a uniform, she is different without it and more so in here. I get sleepy. Solgunn picks up some books from a chair.

"Sit down here," she says. "I've got a bottle of wine, someone gave it to me. We'll make some toddy."

She goes into the kitchen while I doze in the chair. There's a little farm in one of the photographs. A girl with no shoes on stands in front of the house. I can see who it is. Perhaps I fall asleep for a while, there is a rumbling in the stove.

Solgunn comes in from the kitchen with two steaming mugs, and we drink toddy. It's hot and sweet and slightly bitter, and I take big gulps.

"Not so fast," she says, and I think it's because I'm drinking too quickly, but it's because I'm talking,

"I can't understand the half of it," she says. I'm still sleepy, and what I say comes quicker than what I think. I can hear myself telling her about Baron Biegler in the landau at night and the coins he throws to the kids in the street and Grandfather in the byre and Gestapo Jørgensen who hit me in the face and a year later was drowned in the harbour in a mysterious way. And while I talk and think I look at Solgunn who is thin without her coat, not skinny, but slim. She sits on the edge of her chair with her mug in her hand smiling and listening. She has lines in her face. I am not thin, I have brown eyes and large features and curves, like an Eskimo, my mother said once, and I tell her that too.

"Maybe a bit more like a negro," says Solgunn, "only white."

I have a round forehead, and now my hair is short the curls are thicker and more wiry.

"You must have been made for warmer climes," says Solgunn. "Italy or Spain or maybe Morocco."

"I was going to Siberia," I say, "*Jesper* was going to Morocco, my brother, he's there now, but he doesn't write letters. He gets brown after just one day in the sun.'

"Siberia?" says Solgunn.

"Yes."

"It gets cold enough here. Just you wait."

"I'm used to the cold," I say.

"'Maybe you're like Alberte,' she says, 'in Cora Sandel's books. She was always cold before she grew up and went to France. You're aiming in the wrong direction."

I have not read those books, and I don't want to go anywhere now, I want to stay here. I fall asleep again, and when I wake up I'm still in the same chair with a rug over my knees and on the rug is *Alberte and Jakob* by Cora Sandel. It is dark outside now, and I see my face in the window in front of me and Solgunn standing behind me, her hands are on my shoulders, and she moves them up my neck, over the ears and through my hair like a comb. I cannot move, the rug is so heavy.

"Do you mind," I say, but she replies:

"I want to make you warm. Don't you want me to?" She comes round the chair and bends over me, her face covers mine and her fair hair tickles my cheek, I can't see the window any more, my face is gone. I open my mouth slightly and she kisses me. Some women are like that, I am not like that, but if I allow her to kiss me I am sure she will let me sit in this chair as long as I like. She puts her hands round my head, presses it lightly back, and I think, now I can't borrow books any more.

18

I do not remember how long I was ill that time, whether it was days or weeks or even longer, whether I went to the doctor or the doctor came to us, but there were brown bottles on the bedside table and clear glass bottles of pills; I remember Aunt Kari's face in the doorway and the pattern of the wallpaper that had vines in red and turquoise and little ladies with baskets over their arms. I remember I drank a lot of water, and the cold floor when I had to go to the lavatory with my legs shaking and the first dinner after my temperature was normal. The food all came up again because it had been too long since I last ate anything. I watched the day changing through the window on to the courtyard where the shadows rose and fell, rose and fell in a system I could not make out, because sometimes it was quick and sometimes slow, and I have a photograph that Aunt Kari sent me several years later. "My Bergen-Belsen Girl" she had written on the back. I thought that was obscene then, and it is obscene now, but I was thinner than I'd ever been before. I was skinny, not slim, and my round parts had edges on them, and it is true that I looked like some of the photographs in the newspapers the year after the war.

But I came through it and was back in the café before the leaves had fallen from the trees in Kiellands square.

It was dark out there when I arrived and dark when I left, and the wind tore at the trees and people held on to their hats, and the buses were heavier than before; I stood at the window looking out when there weren't many customers and felt the vibration in my body when they drove past. It was as if the glass had grown thinner, or my skin had. On the fourth day he came across the square. It was cold outside and warm inside, and he came in with his coat collar turned up, blew on his hands and rubbed them together while he looked at me and said:

"Have you been ill?"

I make a decision. I walk from Carl Berners square to Grønlandsleiret and on along the street in the dark between the lamps past the Olympen restaurant and the road up to the left beside the little park, to the building with a filling station where the Sportsklub 09 has training quarters upstairs. Vålerenga doesn't have a boxing club so he trains at the 09. But he can't enter boxing contests, you have to be under thirty-two for that.

"It's a pity," he said in the café, "because I'm good," and he didn't blush when he said that. I don't know how good he is, it is hard for me to say, but I walk up the hill with cautious steps. It is October, and the coat Aunt Kari gave me is almost too warm. He asked if I would come and watch, and I said yes, because the nights are long and Solgunn has been to the door and rung the bell twice. She found my address in the lending library list, and when the bell rings I go into the living room and hide behind the curtain looking down on the pavement until she comes out again, and then I see how straight and slender her back is, how straight her hair has been cut below the ears, and she walks quickly up the street, stops suddenly and stands with her arms at her sides and her hands clenched, and I wait, and she does not look back, and then she starts to walk on again.

I go up the stairs and into the boxing hall, and there are only men there, I should have known that. I stand by the wall just inside the door and light a cigarette, and at first no one turns round. I stand quite still thinking this is probably silly, perhaps I should go away, and then they notice the smoke, and a man in a green tracksuit says without looking at me:

"Where did that lady come from?" Another man shrugs his shoulders, and they don't turn round, they have eyes in the backs of their heads and at the same time they're looking at the boxing ring in the middle of the floor where two men in boxing gloves and not much else circle around each other with lowered heads. One of them has just landed a blow on the other, and the one who struck is the man who invited me. His red curls flop about, his body is white in a whirling movement, he has freckles on his back and is powerful and at the same time slim and has lines and curves that constantly change and his feet dance as if they didn't know what it was to stumble. Both of them gleam in the lamplight, and he gets another punch in, there's a dull sound, that hurt, I think, and they stop and my man bends forward with his gloves on his knees and says:

"Bloody hell, did that hurt? Sorry," and it looks as if

he meant it. The other smiles bravely, but it *did* hurt.

"That'll do," shouts the man in the green tracksuit, "go and get showered. Those taking part in the tournament at the weekend line up, and try to keep quiet for once!"

No one has said anything, but out of every nook and cranny come men of my age and still younger in thick sweaters which they slowly pull off, they range themselves in two rows, half-naked and shivering, and the two in the ring go towards the ropes. Then he sees me and waves his glove in the air. Everyone turns. A howl rises to the roof. It fills the room, rolls towards the door, hits the walls and crashes in again, and I press my back against the wall behind me. I'm dumb, I'm not the one I was, and the man in the tracksuit turns and waits, looking me in the eye before he yells:

"SHUT UP!" and silence falls. He smiles, he hates me, and I have never even seen him before.

The man I'm here for comes down between the rows, and it's impossible to see what he is thinking, because he's looking at the floor while he unfastens his gloves and stops right in front of me and says:

"Hold out your hands." I put out my cigarette in an ashtray on the pedestal by the door and do as he says. He pulls the gloves over my hands and bends forward pointing at his chin.

"Hit me here," he says seriously. I hit him lightly on the chin with the hand in the glove and he gives at the knees, squints, clutches his throat and staggers back, takes two steps to the side and falls to the floor. He makes sounds like a dying man. I have to laugh, Jesper could

207

have done that. But no one else is laughing. The man in the tracksuit stares at me, and he's not smiling now, they all look towards the door where I stand and I feel how hard it is to breathe in the room. I pull off the gloves, drop them on the floor and say:

"I'll be outside waiting for *fifteen* minutes."

I stand on the stairs with my hand on the wrought-iron rail until silence has fallen behind the door. I wait. Finally the anger comes. I go back and open the door and slam it as hard as I can, and then I go on down. Out on the pavement I light a fresh cigarette, cross the road and go in among the trees, stand in the shadows and look back at the lights of the filling station and the door to the stairs. I look at my watch. I wait. It starts to snow. It's only October, but it is snowing through the trees and out on the street in the light of the lamps and in front of the filling station it's snowing hard. The snow and the smoke of my cigarette swirls white among the branches above me. I take a few steps, then retrace them again. If I turn my back on the street I just see trees and snow. I am wearing lined snowboots with zips and warm stockings. I try to run. It's fine. I have snow on my coat and snow in my hair and snow on my nose which I blow off, and I run zigzag among the trees with the cigarette in one hand and my coat held tight at my throat with the other. I stop and stay there, hopping up and down. I look at my watch. Before the quarter of an hour is up he comes out. His hair is wet, he sees the snow and smiles, he sees ski slopes and spruce trees and hot soup, he looks at his watch and peers down the street, he looks up the street and down again. But I'm not there. I am miles away, in Vannverks forest gazing over the sea to Norway. I let him wait until he is about to give up, his shoulders sink and he bites his lips, and then I walk out of the shadows and cross the street laughing. He sees me and smiles cautiously.

"It's snowing," he says.

The night is dark and dense and unbelievably white. A car is coming up the hill. The snow flies before the lights and lies so thick on the road that the back of the car slips on the bend from Grønlandsleiret and it pulls itself upwards on wheels that spin and spatter. He turns and looks after it.

"If I had a car I could just have gone," he says, but where would he have gone? He suddenly looks so like an orphan that I take his arm and feel at once that I have never touched him before. I do not understand it. I thought I had, I have thought of it like that, many times. He stiffens, he is dark where he was light before, he is tense and hard as iron under his coat sleeve and I let go before he pulls his arm away.

"Where would you have gone?"

"I don't know. I have been to Örebro in Sweden," he says, "I could have gone to Örebro."

"What did you do there?"

"All the Baptists who make shoes have been to Örebro. There's a school there. But anyway I haven't got a car."

"It's quite easy without one," I say. "I go by bus, you can travel a long way by bus. Or train, you can travel to the Pacific by train." But he still stands there looking after the red rear lights of the car that vanishes up the hill to Galgeberg and Vålerenga and the district where he lives. Perhaps he doesn't want to go anywhere, perhaps he wants to go home. He looks at his watch again.

"Well, I don't want to go home. The last bus for Svartskog leaves in fifteen minutes. We'll catch it if we get it at Gamlebyen."

"Svartskog?"

"Yes. Will you come with me?" He bites his lips again.

"All right," I say. But he didn't say anything about the bus back. When *that* goes. I have no idea where Svartskog is.

We start to walk without speaking, he goes first and I follow, but that's all right, he is quite different now out here in the snow that fills every corner of the world and spreads a blanket over every thought and every house so the town disappears, and I can't see which way we're going. And then he comes to a halt. It has stopped snowing. The air is dark and shining like oil. The bus comes round the corner and I am blinded by its lights, it is in trouble and dares not stop at once, it needs room to brake and sails at an angle in to the pavement further on and opens up its doors. Only one-man buses run so late and we get in at the back and have to walk right down between the seats to the driver to pay. There are very few passengers, but I am too restless to sit down.

"Let's stand at the back," I say.

"It's a long way," he says, "over ten kilometres."

"That doesn't matter."

We go back between the seats to the standing area at

the end one step down, and we hang on to the bar while the bus lurches and shakes away from the lights of the town beside the fjord and the harbour, and there are red and yellow reflections from lanterns and ferries and houses lying close to the water. A big ship glides in among the cranes and comes to a stop. I follow it with my eyes until it disappears behind a promontory and the town is out of sight and only the snow shines white on the road and the trees.

He points up and out of the window on the opposite side. "Ekeberg is up there," he says.

I turn, but I can only see the mountain wall a few metres from the bus.

"I was up there on the summit with a thousand other people watching the airship *Norge* take off. I'll never forget it. It was fantastic. It was in 1926. It was going to Leningrad first and then further north. Nobile was on board, Amundsen was waiting at Spitsbergen. They were going to fly over the North Pole."

"1926," I say. "That was the year I was born." He blushes in the half-darkness, and then he laughs.

"I suppose it was."

The bus turns in from the main road along the fjord, all is dark. We glide through the night, and suddenly there are houses with lights in the windows on both sides of the road, and I might well have lived in a place like that, just as lonely and swallowed up, and then it is dark again, and sometimes I can see the black water between two ridges. We stand at the back without speaking, the bus stops sometimes to let people off, and finally we are the only ones left, but we do not sit down. Just hang on to the bar when there's a sharp swing, and the bus changes down on its way up a steep slope with many bends, and the back is slung around and *we* are slung with it. Then it's straight ahead again, and at last the bus stops, the engine goes quiet and dies, and it's quite obvious that we're not talking. The driver turns round and calls out too loudly:

"Last stop, Svartskog." The back door opens and we get out. There is a shop there with black windows and a farm a little further on and possibly more houses round the bend, but it is mostly dense forest in all directions. He starts to walk along the road, the driver strikes a match inside the bus, it is the only light I see. For a moment I hesitate, then I go up to the front door and knock. It snaps open. The driver leans forward with his cigarette in his mouth.

"Yes?" he says. I stand there staring at him; the narrow tie and uniform cap with its shiny peak and the shadow over his forehead so I cannot see his eyes, and I do not remember what I wanted.

"Yes?" he says again, a bit more sharply, and then I take the packet of cigarettes out of my coat pocket, shake one out and hold it between two fingers. He rattles his matches still sitting down and I stand there, but he does not get up. I have to go up the two steps. He lights a match, it is warm inside the bus, I bend and don't look at his face.

"Thanks," I say and go out again. The door shuts. I'm a bit dizzy, I take a drag and shut my eyes then open them again. I turn round. He is standing fifty metres further on waiting. I take a couple more drags and then throw the cigarette down and walk towards him. Halfway there I stop and look back. The bus has not moved, it stands quiet in the darkness, the cigarette on the ground is still glowing.

We walked for a quarter of an hour along a path through the forest. It was dark, but he knew the way and did not take a single false step, the snow lay on the spruce trees and he called back when I had to be careful and held branches aside so they would not hit my face, and snow fell and hit me on the neck. And then the heavens opened and the moon came out, and we were through the forest. We came out on to a road where the snow lay white without any tracks, and on the other side of the road there was nothing. I went across and on to the edge to look down the steep slope at the water shining black in the light of the moon.

"The Bunnefjord," he said. "Roald Amundsen's house is a few hundred metres on the left, our cabin's just over here on the right."

We went along the road where the gravel crunched under the snow beneath our feet. It was a red-painted timber cabin close to the road behind a fence, and there was a gateway we had to go through first with two big gateposts made up of stones, walled together so they looked as if they had always been together, and *he* had built them, he said, and it took three weeks and two days in bed with a bad back. The cabin looked welcoming even though there was snow heaped up against the windows and streaks of white on the walls, and snow on the roof, and there were big windows looking on to the fjord where you could sit in the evening and watch the sun going down through the trees on the other side of the water.

"Nesodden," he said pointing, but I couldn't see that far in the dark, only the water and the spruces down the slope to the water where there were steps built in and ledges on the bends along the steep path, and right at the bottom there was a canoe upside down on two trestles.

"That's mine," he said.

Inside there was a small lobby with the big windows on the right and then a living room combined with a kitchen where there were piles of wood almost up to the ceiling along one wall and a black wood-burning stove in the middle. It was cold in the lobby, our breath hung white around our faces, and the floor creaked under our feet.

"You need your clothes on in here," he said.

I laughed. "We'd better get some heat going quickly then," I said, and he looked at me, suddenly shy, and then he was eager.

"Heat shall there be," he shouted with hand to fore head in a soldier's salute, "hot as a Turkish bath in no time at all."

"A Turkish bath would be fine," I said, "go ahead."

He pulled kindling from the pile by the wall with such enthusiasm that some of it fell on the floor, and I found a newspaper on a table. I tore the paper into big strips and crushed it up, but he heard what I was doing and turned to shake a forefinger.

"Paper is cheating," he said, "look here," and knelt down in his big coat in front of the stove with a knife in his hand and began to whittle long flakes between his knees until he had a small pile on the floor before him. He laid them in the stove and lit one in his hand and pushed it under the others, and at first the flame was so small he had to blow on it carefully, and then it shot up with a crackle, and he put in a log on each side of the little blaze and pushed them together so the burning space in between was as narrow as a crack, then he shut the stove door again and left the draught vent open so air came in from underneath and blew upwards, and it began to roar and crackle at once. "Dry wood and a good draught, that's what you need," he said proudly, and I clapped my gloves and cried:

"Bravo!" He placed his hand on his chest and bowed so his curls reached the floor.

"Are there any more stoves?" I asked.

"There's one in the loft."

"I must see that." I went quickly up the steep stairs and he followed close behind me. The whole first floor was one room with a little window at one end and beds along both long walls, or actually the ceiling, for the sloping roof went right down to the floor, and there was a faint smell of damp bedclothes like the ones at Vrangbæk, and at the other end there was a small stove on four legs shaped like lions' feet.

"Does it get hot?" I said.

"It gets red-hot."

"Let's get some wood then."

We ran back, he first and I following him, between the beds and downstairs, and we each picked up an armful of wood from the pile by the wall and the knife for whittling and ran up again, we couldn't be quick enough. He knelt down in front of the stove, and it wasn't long before he had done the trick again. Outside the windows it was night now, and the wind blew vaporous white milk against the panes, milk over the forest and the fjord, but in here there were just the two of us and the stoves and the sound of the wood burning behind the black iron and sending waves of heat out into the rooms and into the walls and the timbers that sucked it in. I smelt the scent of wood growing warm, and it made me as white in my head as the whirling night outside, and hungry. We stood in the kitchen with our coats on eating the contents of two tins with one spoon we took it in turns to use, and we laughed, I didn't even notice what I was eating. Soon it was warm enough for us to take off some clothes, his overcoat and my coat, and while he hung his on a hook, I let mine fall to the floor. I took off the sweater I wore underneath and dropped that on the floor too, I unbuttoned my blouse and still felt the cold against my neck. But the heat rose to the ceiling and up to the first floor and there was another stove there. Then I calmly walked across the room and upstairs with his eyes on my back, and at first he stood still, and then he followed, and when he got to the top my blouse was off and my stockings on the floor. I slowly turned round and stood there, me inside my skin, while he was fully clothed, and I cleared my head of every thought I had ever had and let them sink out into my skin till it was painfully taut and shining all over my body, and he *saw* it and did not know what it was he saw. I put my arms round my back and unfastened my bra and slid the straps over my shoulders, and I thought he might be going to weep, but his voice sounded hoarse as he whispered:

"You're lovely," and I answered "Yes," and didn't know if that was true. But it did not matter, for I knew what I wanted and what to say, and his hands were as I'd thought they would be, his skin as soft and his body as hard, and it was so warm around us, and the whole time I smelt the dampness of the bedclothes like the ones at Vrangbæk, and then I just shut my eyes and floated away.

19

I slept, and I dreamed I was in Siberia. There were the great plains with unbroken lines, and a sky and a light as from the dawn of the world, and timbered houses and flocks of birds like a thousand flamingoes that changed into seagulls when they took off and flew and filled the world before they dissolved and were gone. There were herds of horses all of them black, and I was the only rider. We galloped alongside the train, and it was so long I could see no end in either direction. It travelled fast, I felt the horse rising and falling between my legs, and I liked it and wanted to go on like that, but I could not, I had to get over into the train. I rode the horse as close to it as possible and leaned sideways. My hair was long and heavy, it flew out in the wind and back in my face so my eyes stung and the tears ran down, but I caught hold of an iron handle and swung myself over on to the platform at the back of the carriage. It was not difficult, I had seen it in films. I ran into the carriage, but he was not there. The train was empty, the seats empty, and through the window I could see all the pretty horses. The closest was the one I had been riding. Now I saw it was Lucifer, and Jesper was on his back. I had not seen Jesper for four years. I remember the date exactly, the 4th September 1943. I said it aloud. He waved and called, but I could not hear, for the sound of the train on the rails and the sound of the hooves filled the carriage so there was room for nothing else. He waved again and called. I pressed my face to the window but the herd of horses with Jesper in their midst turned away from the train so the distance grew greater and greater until they vanished behind the horizon that was just as sharp and ruler-straight as the train. Now he will fall, I thought.

When I opened my eyes everything was familiar. I blinked and looked straight at the open timbered wall at the end of the room. He slept beside me in the narrow bed. I felt his chest rise and fall next to mine. It was cramped but not uncomfortable. I moved my leg out carefully and quickly turned to look at him. He lay with his curls on the pillow and one forearm over his eyes as if he did not want to see. I picked up the clothes I found on the floor and walked naked downstairs. The stoves were still glowing, but all the same I felt gooseflesh on my thighs and back, and at first I tiptoed but then I put my feet down. That woke me up, and I wanted to wake up. I went out into the room with the big windows and sat on a chair looking out at the fjord between the trees while I dressed. The land on the other side was clearly visible now. There was a boat out on the water, completely still, with a man at each end, and the water shone like silver. They were fishing, their arms rose and fell rythmically, kept still, then began again. All the snow had gone. All the leaves had gone. The night had been windy, now it was still, but the wind had been warm. Drops fell from the roof and everything that was white yesterday was green now and grey, and red on the trees where the rowan berries hung in heavy clusters like decorations someone had put up while I slept.

I looked at the stairs. They were partly lit, in shadow at the top, and I knew I would not go up again. I found my coat on the floor and my snowboots, walked towards the door and opened it carefully so it would not creak, and then I went out. The air was soft on my face. I walked down the path to the gate and out between the big stone gateposts built together so they looked as if they had always been together, and on along the road in the opposite direction from the way we had come the night before. It ran level with the forest at first, and then down a slight slope. On the fjord side there were more cabins beside the road behind fences painted red and white, and in some places it was so steep that I looked straight down on the roofs. The sky was covered with pale grey clouds, or mist, but nevertheless it was easy to breathe, and I walked neither quickly nor slowly, and I felt as if I had no weight.

At the bottom the road ended in a circular space. On the opposite side a bigger road continued in the same direction with large boulders on the fjord side, and another road led up into the forest. There was a kiosk here, it was closed with its windows shuttered, and behind the kiosk was a jetty. It was a big one, you could dance on it if you wanted to, and someone was playing music. I took a few steps on the wide boards that looked shiny and newly scrubbed. There was air in my head and air in my legs and at any moment I might rise and sail away, so I moved carefully as if it was the last dance before the lights went out. And then there was something new. I put my hand between two buttons of my coat and under my sweater and right in to the skin and stroked my stomach.

A lady came out of the nearest house with a bucket in her hand. Only a smooth rock divided us. She wore a scarf round her head knotted over her forehead and came down to the water in my direction. I stopped my dance and stood still to light a cigarette. She had seen me already, she picked up the bucket and embraced it as if it were a man, took a few dancing steps then pirouetted over the rocks laughing.

"Good morning," she called.

I didn't reply, but I raised my hand holding the cigarette and waved. Soon she was so close I could see she was twice my age.

"Isn't it great," she said, throwing out the arm that wasn't round the bucket.

"Yes," I said.

"And the way it snowed yesterday and blew last night, yet today the world is new." She laughed. "I'm getting quite poetic. And you are out dancing. Well, well, not bad. I suppose you haven't one of those to spare?" she said, nodding at the cigarette. I took the packet out of my pocket and she put down her bucket. There were fish in the bucket and a knife for cleaning. I threw the packet across the little channel of water between the jetty and the rock, she caught it perfectly, and then I threw her the matches. She lit one and threw packet and matches back, then squatted down to smoke and look out at the water. She wore over her shoulders a knitted jacket with a multi-coloured pattern, and wellingtons on her feet.

"I've always felt good here. We let our son take over our flat in town and moved out here during the war. He didn't have a home of his own. There was a shortage of everything then. There still is, you know. But I don't want to go back anyway."

"It's great here," I say.

"You're Danish," she said.

"Yes."

"Yes, we wondered about you down there for a while, but when you got going, you really got going."

"29th August 1943," I said.

"That's right. We heard about it from London. Oh, we were tickled pink about that." She smiled at me.

"I'm pregnant," I say.

"Are you? Good for you. You can't beat having kids. The best time of your life, if you ask me. Having kids. If my man agrees, I wouldn't know. Our eldest is twenty-five now." She got up and threw away her cigarette stub. It sputtered and made rings in the water. You could just see brown seaweed waving beneath the surface.

"Thanks for the smoke," she said, "I'd better be getting on. He went out in the boat early, came home with a bucketful and then went back to bed. So it looks as if I've got to do the rest." She laughed again. "Congratulate your husband from me, and tell him not to bother his wife too much."

"I will," I said. "Can I get into town by that road?" I pointed at the big road with boulders along it.

"Yes, you can, but it's a long trek."

I just smiled and waved, and she waved back, bent over the bucket, picked up the knife and the first fish by the tail. I walked back past the kiosk and across the open space. When I had walked along the road for half an hour a car stopped and offered me a lift, and when I arrived in town it was still morning.

There's a slanting yellow light over the town, the mist has lifted and dissolved and everything is clear and yet mild as if it were early spring before the leaves come out and not yet autumn. The trees on Kiellands square are bare, they look as if they're waiting for something other than me when I go up Uelandsgate. The air is as bright as glass and leaves everything sharply defined; the eyes of the man sprinting towards the bus stop, the smile of the girl with a pram in the other direction, I see a squirrel far away in one of the trees. The town was not like this before, not so clean and not so new, but I have no use for it any more, and that is not even sad.

I don't walk quickly, nor slowly, I still feel the lightness and get to the café an hour late, Aunt Kari stands behind the counter watching the door. She puts her head on one side and questions without speaking, and I do not answer, just look suitably mysterious and ask:

"Can I use the sink in the kitchen?" and she nods towards the door. I go in and have a thorough wash with the door shut and come out again with the white waitress's apron tied round my waist. The sun shines in through the windows. They could do with a polish. I go straight over to the only breakfast customer and ask if he has had enough, if there is anything more he would like. He turns to look at me and smiles. I've never seen him before.

"Maybe," he says, stretching his lips over his teeth like Humphrey Bogart, but his hair is thinning and his cheeks are chubby.

"What would you like?" I ask.

"I don't know, maybe you do?"

"Haven't a clue," I say. I pick up his cup and plate and the half-full ashtray and everything I can find and put it on a tray without looking at him. He scratches his neck, the table is cleared, and I carry everything into the kitchen. I wait five minutes, and when I look out he has gone.

For the rest of the day I walk restlessly from the counter to the tables and back again, I am obsessed with crumbs and dust, I clear away and straighten curtains, Aunt Kari says I am annoying the customers.

"For God's sake sit down and have a fag," she says, but I cannot. I stand at the window looking out, but I'm not looking for anything special.

"Anyone would think you had wanderlust," says Aunt Kari.

That night we see a red light above Kiellands square. It was not there before, and we think it has something to do with the sunset. But it is on the wrong side, it flashes in the wrong windows, and we go on with what we are doing, and then the fire engines arrive. Salomon's Shoe Factory is on fire. We go out on the pavement, people come from all sides, some on foot, others cycling. A bus stops, the doors snap open, the passengers stream out and most of them run across the square to get as near the flames as possible, but we stay where we are outside the café.

"Good God," says Aunt Kari, "I hope everyone escaped, we are going to lose some customers, though. Especially one." She turns towards me, I can feel it, but I do not look at her.

"It may well be he's not even there," I say.

"What do you know about that?"

"A bit," I say.

The glow above the square gets stronger, and at the same time it's strangely quiet. We watch cars glide up and shadows running to and fro against the red, quickly and jerkily as in a silent film.

No lives are lost. No one is hurt either, but the factory is ruined and the machinery burned out, so production will move to another part of town until a new factory is built, and that may take a long time. None of the workers come to the café any more. It's too far away, and there are other cafés.

The days go by, and I go with them, but I do not count them. I wait. It is a flowing feeling. I don't read books any more. I work in the café or sit on a chair and leaf through a paper or stand at the window looking out. My mother doesn't write any more. "If you don't write, I shan't," she said in the last letter, and she means it. She is iron. I am iron too. I don't write. I have nothing to say to her. I go out in the car with Aunt Kari. We go for long trips on Sundays with a map and a picnic. She has a permit to buy petrol because the Citroën is registered for the café, it's a commercial car, and even though petrol is hellishly dear she does not lift an eyebrow when she pays. We drive to the Lier hills outside Drammen, along the tops where we look out over the fjords. We drive to a farm near Årnes where she has friends, and I don't know where she met them, but they are happy for us to come and give us cakes. I go on my own to the byre and along the row of cows and feel the warmth of their bodies streaming towards me and stroke their backs and say words to them only they can hear. We go to Bingsfossen at Sørum early one morning. I sleep most of the way. Aunt Kari stops the car just above the suspension bridge, and we walk down to the river on the flat rocks. The water roars down the rapids and sprays a shower of drops over our hair and coats, and there are piles of timbers on the bank with the owners' mark cut into the end of each log. The whole area and my coat smell of timber for several days. It's chilly beside the river, but Aunt Kari wants to make coffee on an open fire, and I shiver and get the coffee pot from the car, I am still sleepy, but I make use of what I have learned and get a little fire going.

I serve the coffee standing. We clasp our hands round the mugs and blow into the warmth while we look at the rushing river. Aunt Kari smokes a thin cigar and stands nearest to the river with her back to me, and that back is so broad, and we have done it all as she wanted, the river roars and thunders so loud we can hardly talk, the coffee is piping hot on our palms, and only then do I realise she has been to all these places before, with someone else, in the same car. She turns and smiles. She has a scarf round her head and sunglasses and a big black coat. She looks like a matron, the mother of many children. I smile back, we have a fine time. I take a big mouthful of coffee, and suddenly it's bitter and fills every hollow of my body, nausea shoots up my throat, my stomach turns over and everything comes up all over the rocks in front of me. I'm not prepared, I drop the mug and mess my coat, the china splinters and breaks around us. I bend down and vomit again.

"Bloody hell," I say.

"What's wrong with you?" Aunt Kari says. She hurries over the rocks with a handkerchief and wipes my mouth and the front of my coat and looks me in the face:

"You've gone quite green."

"I felt so sick. That coffee must be bad."

"There's nothing wrong with the coffee that I could taste."

"I think I need to sit down for a while," I say.

"You go up and sit in the car. We've finished here now."

I don't quite know what it is we have finished, but I do as she says, go and sit in the car, and feel better at once. The only thing I smell is the timber, and it is insistent, but if I breathe carefully through my nose I can keep the nausea down. Aunt Kari rinses out the coffee pot and puts out the fire with water from the river, then comes heavily up beside the bridge and puts the coffee pot in the little boot.

"How are you feeling?" she says in the car on the way back to Oslo. We drive with the window half open.

"Fine," I say, and in a way that is true.

One day there is a letter for me on the kitchen table. It's leaning against a cup where I shall see it at once. I see it at once. It has stains and stamps with intertwining letters. I open it and read:

Dear Sistermine,

it runs,

when you get this letter I shall probably be home in Denmark again. The mail takes a long time, I'm told. Mum sent me your address, and that letter had been on its way for centuries. I have been here a long time now, longer than I'd intended. The people I was with left a couple of weeks ago, or maybe more. I'm not quite clear about it. They took the boat across the straits of Gibraltar to Spain. But I shan't set foot in that country now,

he writes:

not with that butcher Franco as dictator. On the way south we took a train to Marseilles and a ship from there. In the harbour before we sailed I saw a woman I'll never forget. I took her photograph, I couldn't resist it but she didn't see me. She stood on the quay shouting and weeping beside the gangway, there were people everywhere, French police with hard black peaked caps

Arabs on their way home, some in djellabas, others with Turkish fezzes on their heads, and Americans with white tropical helmets playing at Africa already. She didn't see any of them, she stood with closed eyes behind her spectacles facing the boat, and she beat herself on the throat so her cries came out in short bursts rather like the way we played at Indians when we were small. I swear, Sistermine, it was the most horrible noise I have ever heard. And she looked like Mother. Just as small, the same grey hair and the same grey coat and hat. I looked around to see who the strange screams could be for. By the rail a few metres away stood a man, younger than me, almost a boy. He stared at her. His face was like stone, his hair cut short all over his head, and it was impossible to guess what he was thinking. Then he turned and walked across the deck without looking back. She didn't see him either, her eyes were still closed and she was still beating her throat and crying out, and I had the feeling I had that time I was on the way over to Hirsholmene and found the cap on the ice. That I had to turn round. Wasn't that strange? But Morocco is not Denmark. I am certain the young man was on his way to join the Foreign Legion.

He writes:

Sistermine, I have seen it all, all the places in the book we had at home; Marrakech, Fes, Meknés, Kasba, do you remember how I used to say those names aloud, and they were exactly as I knew they would be, but in colour! Terracotta and brick and yellow sand and red sand and blue mountains, and the people we called the blue men who came with their camels and horses to the market at Marrakech weren't blue, they were like you after a summer with lots of sun. And the Berbers from the mountains were whiter than me and some were blonde with blue eyes. You and I never had that. So who is Aryan in this world? They were sceptical towards me because in appearance I looked French to them, and I was sceptical towards them because I knew Franco used Berbers in the Fascist army. They were proud and could fight like fiends for their freedom, but probably they weren't so fussy about others' if the money was good. They have a saying which goes: kiss the hand you can't cut off. Bloody hell, say I,

it runs, and he writes:

On the way from Al-hajeb to Meknés by bus a few days ago we stopped at the foot of a mountain, and there was a tent and a woman with small children and some black goats. She was tall and beautiful with tattoos on her face, and she had a scarf on her head with coins or medallions sewn to the edges so close together they jingled when she walked and jingled when when she bent over the goats. I had to go up to her. I had been so thirsty the whole way, we had travelled for hours, it was as hot as the ante-room of hell, and I said to her in French, *"J'ai soif!"* and she understood that. She picked up a wooden bowl and went and milked one of the goats straight into the bowl and gave it to me. It was very kind of her, and I took a big mouthful. Say thanks for me to the cows at Vrangbæk, if they're still alive. It tasted terrible. Maybe that's why I'm lying here now, in a little guest house near the Socco Grande in Tangiers. I've been feverish for a couple of days, but I think I was a bit better this morning. The son of the house runs errands for me and tells stories at full speed in a blend of Spanish and French and a dose of Moghrebi. It sounds like a new language. He falls to his knees and laughs aloud when he gets to the point, and I don't understand a thing. He's twelve. Tomorrow I'm sure I'll be on my feet again. I need to be actually, I've booked passage on a freighter to Nice leaving in two days from now. I'll work my way over. From there it's the train home with the last of my money.

He writes:

Sis, there's so much to tell you, but it must wait till we meet, and that will be soon. Then you must tell me everything too. I haven't seen you since that time in the harbour. I forgot the photograph, do you remember? I realised it in Sweden. Everything went so fast, it was a crazy time. And then you weren't there when I got home.

Now I must sleep, and when I wake up I'll be better and I'll go out and fetch the presents I've bought. I've hidden them in a safe place. At the moment I don't trust anyone.

20

Aunt Kari drove me to the quay. It was winter again. There was snow in the streets and silence and early dark. Between the houses in Storgata, Christmas decorations had been put up all the way from Ankertorget to Kirkeristen, and we drove down Skippergata and out by the big warehouse and on beneath the castle where it was shadowy beside the wall and gloomy like *Quai des Brumes* with Jean Gabin. A new ship lay at Vippetangen. The *Melchior* had gone, this one was called *Vistula*. The Vistula was a river in Poland and the ship had sailed between Gdansk and Copenhagen with Polish refugees until quite recently.

"Gdansk was Danzig when the town was German," said Aunt Kari, but I did not need to be told that. We walked from the car to the departure hall past some taxis with open boots, the drivers were getting baggage out. All red in the face they walked to the entrance with a bag in each hand and one under each arm and put them down in rows, but I carried my own suitcase. The ship was quietly waiting when we went out on the other side of the hall. It was smaller than the *Melchior* with fewer decks and the gangway was just a plank with railings like a well-made chicken ladder. People were walking up the plank, and I wanted to get on board as fast as I could, but Aunt Kari took my arm and said:

"So far so good, my dear. Now, you mustn't get seasick."

I put down the suitcase.

"I've never been seasick before. I'm really fine."

"Have a schnaps on an empty stomach just before you eat, it usually helps. Here's a small contribution," she said, pushing a note into my hand.

"Thanks, but I'm sure everything will go well."

"Maybe it will, but you must remember to be careful, mustn't you." She was still holding my arm and squeezing it hard, and when she realised that she blushed and let go. I stroked her cheek.

"Aunt Kari, everything will be all right now," I said, picking up my case, I was impatient and feeling bad about it.

"I wonder," she said quietly, and she had tears in her eyes, and then I couldn't say any more, even though I knew it would be a long time until we saw each other again. And then I went on board.

She stood on the quay until the ship was under way and I stood on deck, and for a moment I was certain she was going to take out a cigar, but she only raised her hand, turned and walked through the hall and out on the other side where the taxis had gone away and she got into the Citroën and drove off. I looked at the note I held in my hand. It was a hundred kroner. I could buy myself schnaps for months with that.

I didn't have a berth but a hammock in a section of the

233

ship without port-holes two stairways down from the superstructure in the stern. It was pitch dark when I went in with my suitcase in one hand and a blanket I had been given in the other, and I put down the case to find the light switch. When the light came on I saw there were more suitcases and bags in there, but only one hammock was occupied, and that someone turned round and said:

"Put that light out, for Christ's sake!"

"In a moment," I said, "I just want to stow my luggage."

I went over to a free hammock next to the person, who was a lady, put my blanket into it and the suitcase underneath.

"I'm feeling so ill, you see," she said, and then I saw her face. She didn't look well. She screwed up her eyes and pulled her mouth into a tight line. She was younger than me.

"Is there anything I can do, shall I fetch help?"

"Oh, no, I'm just so damn seasick. It's the same every time."

"Seasick now? We're not at Drøbaksundet yet."

She opened her eyes. "Aren't we? Damn it, I thought we were long past that. I can't have slept for more than five minutes."

"There won't be much sea running till we're past Færder lighthouse. Besides, it's dead calm."

"Is it?" She raised her head and looked around her. She had red hair like Rita Hayworth in technicolor, it lay around her head in a huge tangle.

"You're Danish, aren't you," she said. "Are you on your way home?"

"You could say that. An old aunt of mine says the best remedy for seasickness is a schnaps on an empty stomach just before you eat."

"All very well for *her* to say that. *I'm* broke."

"But I'm not. May I treat you?"

"Thanks for the offer," she said, getting carefully out of the hammock and putting her feet on the floor to see if it moved. It did not.

"I'm Klara," she said.

It was dark outside the windows of the cafeteria, but we could sometimes glimpse the snow where the fjord was narrow, and the lamps in houses right down by the water and a car on a bridge with its lights on, and mostly we saw our own faces in the glass. Klara had brushed her hair till it shone and stood out like mine would have done if it had not been cut short, and she had a sweet face with fair skin which must have been freckled in summer. She raised her glass with the clear schnaps and said:

"Farewell, Birthplace of Giants; I'm sick of it. Shall I tell you who I was named after?"

"You may as well," I said.

"Clara Zetkin. D'you know who that is?"

"Yes. She was a German communist."

"Right. German communist and friend of Lenin. They wrote letters to each other. She was a giant. My father is a giant too. He's a communist at Aker Mekaniske Verksted. He makes speeches with his fist clenched at club meetings. My boyfriend is smashing, in a few years he'll be a great giant too. It's not that I'm against them at all, but I'm fed up. They won the war single-handed. They can't talk about anything else. And then *I* have to make coffee. So I picked up my hat and left, as they say. Anyway for a while. Now they can make the coffee themselves. I'm going to Hirtshals in Jutland to clean fish."

I pictured Rita Hayworth in a fish delivery hall. It didn't seem so daft.

"We had a picture of Lenin," I said. "That's to say, my brother had. In a shack we built on the shore. It may still be hanging there."

"Are you a communist?"

"No, I'm a syndicalist."

"Ah ha. Then we'd better not discuss the Spanish war. Or there'll be trouble."

I laughed. "No, better not." I said. "Skål." Then each of us emptied our glasses into each of our empty stomachs before we ate the rissoles that were the dish of the day, and the only one.

After Færder I was the one who was ill. We had gone down to bed and fallen asleep at once, and when I woke up I heard violent creaking and the sound of the sea beating along the sides of the ship and someone snoring in the darkness. It was not Klara. I felt the nausea rising and didn't know whether it was the schnaps we had drunk or the bad air or the sea against the ship that lifted and dropped all the space around me, but I had to get out. I found my coat in the heap of clothes and the door in the dark and went out into the blinding light of the staircase and up the stairway, leaning first against one wall and then the other with the ship's movements, and right up on deck. It was dark out there with throbbing sounds. The weather had changed. There was a shrieking wind and white foam in the air and a sudden slash of drops on my face. With my coat tightly around me I went over to the other side of the deck so I had the wind behind me and vomited over the railing. "How kind of you to feed the fish," Jesper would have said. I wiped my mouth and walked backwards until my back was against the wall of the superstructure, held on tight and stared out into the grey-black spray where the crests rushed along, and I stood there till I felt better and so long that my teeth began to chatter and then a bit more.

When I went down darkness filled the space so densely that I felt the air like cloth against my face, I had to support myself along the wall and feel my way to the empty hammock. I leaned against it to swing myself up, and that was hard enough with the light on and dead calm, and even more difficult now.

"Is that you?" whispered Klara. "Are you ill?"

"I must be."

"I'm quite all right, isn't that weird?" she said. "I was always sick before. It must be those schnapses."

I did not reply. If I lay right back with my eyes open and did not move, I didn't feel too bad.

"Hey," whispered Klara, "can I ask you one thing?"

"Yes, of course."

"Are you going to have a baby?"

"Why do you ask that?"

"Because you keep on stroking your stomach, and I thought, unless that lady has a bloody awful pain in her stomach, she must be expecting a baby. My sister did the same thing when she was pregnant. She didn't even realise she was doing it."

I didn't realise it either. I stroked my stomach in the dark and felt quite sure there was something there, and I had been so confident the whole time and so full of expectation, but now I could not remember why. Maybe it was the night, and this darkness and the sea out there with no light from anywhere, only grey black in one huge abyss and the ship so frail and weightless and far away from everything.

"Yes," I said, "I'm going to have a child."

"That explains everything," said Klara, "now you mustn't bother me any more. I need to sleep." Then she was quiet and perhaps she slept, and the creaking went on and the sound of the sea thumping against the ship, but the hammock followed gravity more than the movements of the boat, and it was like hanging in the middle of a wheel with the whole world spinning round and round, and I lay quite still.

I was awake and up on deck before Skagen. It was still dark with a pale grey streak in the direction of Sweden, and I stayed there till I saw the lighthouse in front, and I stood by the rail as we passed and let myself be dazzled. The sea was calmer now, the seagulls following us hung over the ship completely still and grey and unmoving as if they were tied to invisible threads, and when the beam of light came they were suddenly white and so close that if I stood on tiptoe I was sure

I could stroke the feathers under their breasts.

I stood there until the lighthouse disappeared to the north and only the flashes came each time the beam pointed at the ship's course, and then I went into the cafeteria. I sat there for an hour before Klara came up with her hair in chaos, and the ship turned towards land round Hirsholmene, and I saw the lights of the town and Pikkerbakken faintly in the grey light behind the houses and the lights of the breakwater, red and green alternately, and the masts in the fishing harbour and the corn silo and the church with the bell like a golden spot in the tower. The tugboat came thumping towards us from inside the harbour, and Klara sat down beside me and said:

"I get really melancholy when I arrive at a new place like this. Don't you?"

"Not exactly," I said, "this is my town. I was born and brought up here."

"So you're home, then."

Home, I thought, where is that. I gazed at the quay and the few people there, but it was still too far away to distinguish one from another in the grey light that made all the colours melt together.

"Then you will be met and everything. I'm quite alone, I am. But that's what I wanted, of course."

"We'll see," I said.

There was no one there to meet me. I didn't know what to think. Everything was familiar, and everything was strange. Klara walked away from the ship with me. We each carried our suitcases along the inner quays where fish boxes with holes in them were immersed in the water with the live catch inside, and two fishermen pulled the net from its roll in their boat and out over the quay in one big fan, I saw there were tears in it and loose threads in several places. They wore big boots and oilskin trousers with wide braces and thick jumpers and caps of the same material. One of them had bare hands. It was cold, and they were painfully red and swollen from the freezing wind and water, and I felt uncomfortably neat and different in Aunt Kari's coat as we walked past. Klara turned and stared and could not stop staring and almost walked backwards up to the Cimbria Hotel.

"Christ. I'll be meeting that sort of bloke every day. Just look at them," she said, but I didn't want to turn round.

"I've seen them before," I said. We were almost at Lodsgade, and I felt like stopping or walking past. It was confusing.

"Yeah, of course you have," said Klara.

We turned up the street and walked past the Færgekroen which was dark and closed and then on to the sign which should read: Herlov Bendiksen – Glazier, but it did not. It read: Konrad Mortensen – Everything in glass and frames, and it came so abruptly that it almost made me cry. It was dark in the dairy shop, and dark in the little room beside it, but there was light in the living room on the first floor. I stood still for a moment, Klara looked the way I was looking, and then I went on up to Danmarksgade and stopped on the corner and pointed:

"The railway station is five blocks that way and then up to the left into Kirkegade. You'll see it at once. *I'm* not going any further now."

Klara put down her suitcase on the pavement, clasped her arms round me and gave me a big hug. She had perfume on. After a few weeks of cleaning fish *that* would change.

"I don't really want to leave you," she said, "you suddenly looked so sad."

"I'm fine. Now I'm going home and all that."

"Of course you are." She laughed. "I'm not, luckily. Maybe we'll meet again. We're in the same country, at least."

"We probably will," I said.

"Thanks for the schnapses. They gave me a real buzz."

"You're welcome."

She walked backwards up the street for a few steps waving one glove, and I waved back, took a firm grip of the suitcase handle and went down Lodsgade again and into the entrance to No 2.

It was quiet on the staircase. I put the suitcase beside the door leading into the dairy shop. I pushed it ajar and looked in. It was still dark in there, but I saw the clock on the wall. It was past eight. That was odd. The light should be on now and early customers with rolls in paper bags on their way in to buy milk for breakfast coffee. The door of the room at the other end was closed, and no sounds came from it. I took a few steps into the shop and stood there behind the counter on the black and white tiles. I looked at the door for a long time, then I went back again. I left the suitcase standing there and went and sat down on the step in front of the shop and lit a cigarette. It didn't taste good, but I stayed there until it was finished. A man cycled past, he stared at me and went on staring until his head had turned right round and he almost fell off and had to put one foot down. I stubbed out the cigarette on the edge of the step, stood up and went in again and up the steep winding stairs without the suitcase and without making too much noise, but I did not tiptoe either. It smelled of coffee and faintly of cigar as it had always done. The door of the living room was open but it was silent in there. I heard the tick of the pendulum clock. I put my head in to look. They both sat in their chairs by the window, and between the chairs was the lighted lamp and the small table in dark wood and glass where the missionary journals lay in piles. But neither of them was reading.

"Hi, it's me," I said. "You're so quiet in here."

They turned and looked towards the door where I stood. I had only been home once in almost three years, but they looked at me as if I were either a total stranger or had just been down for a couple of minutes to fetch a bottle of milk. At length my father tried to smile, and that was strange too, he hardly ever smiled, and anyway he didn't manage to, and my mother's eyes were blue, blue, blue.

"Where's Jesper?" I asked.

"Jesper is in Morocco," my mother said in a low voice.

"That is not right. I had a letter two weeks ago and then he was about to come home, and that letter had

242

been on the way for just as long. So that *isn't* right."

My father took hold of both armrests to push himself up, his back was as curved as a half moon and his jaws protruded and his grey hair was combed back hard. How come it was grey? It was not like that before. Then he changed his mind and sank down again. He said:

"What she means is that Jesper is in Morocco because he is dead. He never came home."

I did not understand. We had made an arrangement. He was taking a boat to Nice and then the train from there with the last of his money. A child could manage that.

"It isn't possible," I said and took out the letter I had kept in my pocket for two weeks, but my father had a letter too. He leaned forward and passed it to me. It had been on top of the missionary journals. I opened the envelope. It was a brief notice on official paper. At the top it said Tangiers, 15 November. The rest was in Spanish or French, but I could not focus, and I understood nothing. At the bottom on the white part a few lines were pencilled in Danish. I read them.

"We had it translated," said my father.

I gave him back the letter, and he took it as if it were glass.

"It isn't true," I said.

He looked down and sat like that until he finally raised his eyes and then they were different, he clenched his lips, the skin was taut around his eyes. I had been home for fifteen minutes, perhaps twenty, and they had been sitting in those bloody chairs the whole time, and I had been standing on the floor leaning against the dining

table he had made in the workshop. He had made everything in this room, table and chairs and the cupboard by
the wall, he had even rebuilt the piano. The lid of the
keyboard was open with the hymn sheets out. She must
have kept on with her playing and singing in the evenings
and far into the night, and my father had either gone out
of his mind or submitted and been saved. And then
everything disintegrated into small pieces with sharp
edges, I could hear it splitting and crashing around me, it
cut into my numb palms when I stroked my stomach,
and my mother who had said nothing for a long time
looked at my hands, rose from her chair and said coldly:

"Are you expecting a child?"

"Yes," I said.

"And can you show me your wedding ring?" The blue
gaze met mine, and I looked into hers, but there was
nothing there.

"What wedding ring?" I said, but she did not reply.
She walked round me until she stood with her back to the
piano. Above the piano Jesus was sitting by the light of
the moon on the Mount of Olives, deep in thought,
tortured in his hour of doubt. The moon was on its way
behind a cloud. Soon it would be dark. Shall, shall not, he
thought. My mother took off her spectacles and put them
on the table, and her eyes grew even bigger. She said:

"How dare you come into the house of sorrow in this
way? Have you no shame?" Her hands were clasped in
front of her, and I *saw* the flaming sword. I felt it grow
within me, an emptiness like ash in the mouth. I licked
my lips, but it did not help.

I turned to my father. He still sat in his chair looking down at his lap. I stared at him until he had to raise his eyes, and he shook his head like an old man and turned away and looked into the wall. He had nothing to give, and I would not beg. I went out of the room and down the stairs, picked up my suitcase from beside the door and went out through the entrance and away from that house.

21

I had lived in that town for twenty years and never been out to Læsø. Few of us had. In our family only our father had been there that once when he had been looking for work as a carpenter, and he did not tell us anything about it when he came home. But Læsø was easy to get to once you had decided on it, and at the same time it was invisible from the mainland.

The first thing that struck me when I went out there by boat was that I could look over the water back at the town. Not only Pikkerbakken, but the line of rust-red roofs and the church tower and all the high points even on a day when the weather was not completely clear. And I who wanted to get away, now it seemed as if someone was keeping an eye on me, and I could not see who it was. But after a few weeks that ceased to matter. Nothing mattered.

Marianne's uncle was her father's brother, and he agreed that I should stay with him until the child was born, and I was welcome to stay on as long as I was useful. He was a carter too. One of two on Læsø. He also kept sheep. Twenty ewes that were out in the summer and near the buildings in winter, and it was Ingrid's job to look after them. Ingrid was his wife. I was to help her. There wasn't much snow that winter, but it was cold and there was not much for them to eat on the heather-covered